Off the Grid

by

Karyn Good

Off the Grid

Cover Art by *Tina Lynn Stout*

The Wild Rose Press, Inc.
PO Box 708
Adams Basin, NY 14410-0708
Visit us at www.thewildrosepress.com

Publishing History
First Crimson Rose Edition, 2014
Print ISBN 978-1-62830-217-2
Digital ISBN 978-1-62830-218-9

Published in the United States of America

Casual relationships weren't her thing. Once she'd yearned for more. For the commitment other women scoffed at. Then she'd learned her lesson. It didn't mean she didn't crave family. She refused to ask about the woman from his office. It was none of her business. Neither was he. But renewed determination to resist him didn't mean he wasn't getting to her.

No soft music played. The dim lighting was courtesy of an unlit dingy hallway. The smell of antiseptic and desperation laced the air. It didn't matter. Sophie wanted to meet his challenge. She didn't want to dodge. Or object. She wanted to kiss the hell out of Caleb Quinn.

So she stepped back. "I can't do this with you. I need to know I matter. That I'm the only name on your list."

Caleb took her face in his warm hands. "Sophie, right now there is no one else but you."

She wrapped her hands around his wrists and tugged them away. "But there's a long line behind me and I'm choosing not to join the queue."

"Don't." He refused to let go of her hands when she tried to release them, brought them up between them. "Don't toss this aside."

"I don't do casual."

"There won't be anything casual about it."

Praise for *BACKLASH* by Karyn Good

"Chase and Lily are made for each other."

~The Romance Reviews

Dedication

For Josh,
who always takes the time to care

Chapter One

Dr. Sophie Monroe lifted her face to the cold sting of falling snow. The flakes cooled her heated cheeks. Their fresh scent cleansed her mind of the day's battles. On the ground it covered the everyday debris of crack vials and castoff condoms. Litter from the urgent business dealings conducted in the shadowed alley behind her clinic. In the waning light of the gathering storm she studied the dark doorways relieved to find them empty.

Car keys in hand, Sophie ignored the angry shouts drifting down from the corner of Hastings and Gore. Further proof Christmas struggled to find its way to the Downtown Eastside of Vancouver. Here the fight to survive didn't take a vacation. The impossible expectations of the holidays only made difficult conditions worse. The taste of futility, bitter and unfamiliar, flooded up her throat. It spilled into her mouth. There wasn't enough spit in the world to rinse the taste away. She refused to make a meal of it.

It was Christmas Eve. She had a party to attend, donations to secure. Memories to elude.

She trudged through the slushy snow to her beat-up Dodge Dart. Two hours until her attendance was required at Carson Cooper's annual Spirit of Christmas fundraiser. Very glitzy. Very high end. And so not her thing. This year's theme was Silent Night, Safe Night with all of tonight's lovely proceeds benefiting one of her favorite charities, Safe Night's Refuge. She was the guest speaker and seeker of funds. Safe Night was one of the few drop-in missions providing accommodation to entire families. It was money they desperately needed. Alleviating the effects of poverty didn't come cheap. Too bad tonight's deal came with an escort. Caleb Quinn, newly minted partner and shining star, was charged with introducing her around.

She needed to get home, shave her legs, pluck her eyebrows, whiten her teeth, and any number of other time-consuming beauty rituals she often ignored. The little black dress she'd bought to kick the oh-so-urbane Caleb Quinn's ass required no less effort. Time for some screw-you couture. If he was very, very lucky she'd refrain from stabbing him with her five-hundred-dollar-a-plate fork.

Cheered despite the freezing temperatures she retrieved her ice-scraper from the trunk of her car. She didn't enjoy games and he was toying with her. Flirt, impress, and conquer. His lean good looks a tool he wielded against resistance. Less polished than your average affluent lawyer type, his dark brown hair waved down to within a half an inch of too long. He brushed it back from his forehead leaving his face clear for admiring. At six foot something he towered over her. But most people did. She compensated for her lack of height by not giving a shit.

Through the spotty, dim light of late afternoon she caught sight of a dark, hooded figure shuffling in her direction. Sophie's frozen fingers gripped her ice-scraper. It didn't take long to recognize the quick steps, the hunched shoulders. Relief battered at her heart.

She'd given up on finding her in time for Christmas.

"Marnie." She'd spent the last six months searching for her, using her limited spare time to scour Marnie's usual haunts. Nothing.

"I need your help." Marnie wasn't big on conversation at the best of times. Judging by her lack of coat, gloves, or boots to protect against the worsening weather conditions, now was not a good time. She shifted from foot to foot stirring the snow up and over her ratty sneakers. No eye contact. All bad signs.

"What kind of help?" Sophie knew better than to reach out and touch her, especially when she suspected the older woman was off her meds. She didn't want to send her scurrying back into the blizzard.

Marnie motioned to someone in the gray of the shifting shadows, and Sophie tensed. A woman limped toward them clutching her huge belly, dark stains soaked her faded jeans. Alarmed, Sophie glanced at Marnie who held out a hand to the mystery woman, her fingers outstretched, beckoning. The woman stumbled, and they both rushed to her aid, Marnie one step ahead of her. She wrapped an arm around her friend. Sophie tried to hide her shock. Marnie never voluntarily touched anyone. Ever.

She pointed at Sophie. "She's in labor. You're a doctor. Help her."

"Steady. One step at a time. Let's get you inside." Sophie braced the woman's other side. She latched onto Sophie's arm. The hood of her ratty jacket slipped down. Her dirty blonde hair was tied back with a bit of string. Dark circles framed red-rimmed eyes. Fear filled those huge eyes, her mouth tightening against the pain. *So young.* Sophie hid her dismay by rubbing a hand over the girl's back. She kept her voice soft. "It's going to be all right. Can you tell me your name?"

"Her name is Kellie." Marnie's answer was reluctant. Sophie didn't like it. Suspicion was an old friend when it came to Marnie. The girl's identity worried her, the whole situation was too desperate, too furtive. Even for Marnie's manic style. Marnie had friends, but she didn't do friendly. So, why now? Why this girl?

She nudged them forward. "We'll get Kellie inside then I'll call an ambulance."

"No." Marnie glared across Kellie's head at her. "Just you."

No way. If anything went wrong she was on her own. Kellie twisted to hold onto Sophie. A rush of pain bent her over. The wind whipped up the fallen snow, they all braced against it. "She needs to get to a hospital before she has this baby in the street."

"Marnie." Kellie straightened, held up a shaking hand. "Please, I can't do this without help."

Distracted, Kellie slipped on a patch of snow covered ice. Sophie struggled to keep them upright. "The parking lot isn't the place to discuss it. Let's get you into the clinic where it's warm and dry. I'll assess the situation and we'll go from there."

"No one else but you needs to know she's here," demanded Marnie.

Sophie ignored the punch of anxiety. Put aside her need for answers. No one rushed Marnie. "Let's all calm down. We'll figure it out inside. The storm's getting worse and we're risking complications we don't need the longer we stand out here arguing."

Neither of them were dressed for the weather.

Sophie pressed tight to Kellie. Her shivers rippled through both of them. Who knew how long they'd spent outside or how far they'd walked? Sophie urged Kellie forward. She needed to access Marnie's situation too. "How about you? Are you okay?"

Marnie's whole body stiffened, ready to deflect. Her chin came up. "I'm fine. Don't worry about me."

Yeah, right. She'd heard it all before. Believing her was a miracle Sophie had never quite pulled off. She didn't look fine. She'd lost weight she could ill afford to lose. Everything she wore was frayed around the edges, including her usual smirk. Even though she did a good job of hiding it, Sophie caught a peek of the dirty white cast covering her right wrist.

"Are you sure?" But a sudden gust of wind scattered her words. She braced. Her hair blew across her eyes, cold filled her throat. She bent into it and concentrated on moving them toward the door. On a brief moment of respite, Marnie spared a second to wipe the melted snowflakes from Kellie's pale cheek. Bitterness, petty and frustrating, welled up in her gut. Kellie meant a great deal to Marnie. In a way Sophie craved but never managed.

Deep worry etched lines around Marnie's pinched mouth. She glared across at Sophie. "Just do your thing and get this kid out of her."

"Marnie, don't." Kellie shuddered in their arms.

Thank God the door was less than four feet away. They needed to get inside but even behind the doors of her clinic there were limits to what she could deal with, and if things went wrong…

"Only you." Trust Marnie to pick up on her concerns. Nothing got by her. Marnie let go of Kellie and blocked their route to the door. "Promise me."

Sophie buckled under Kellie's stiff weight but refused to give into Marnie's demand. "That's not how it's going to work. This is a clinic, not a hospital. We don't deliver babies. I will be calling an ambulance. I won't risk her or her child's life."

"You're not calling the shots here." The jagged scar dissecting the right side of Marnie's face twisted with her warning.

"Whether you call the shots or I call the shots doesn't change the facts."

"You can't refuse to help her."

"Please, stop," whispered Kellie.

"No, I can't, nor will I. You should know better than that." When had she ever refused to help? Or denied Marnie anything? Her strategy had led them to this emergency-style showdown in a dirty alley. She resorted to threats knowing it would do no good. "But don't bother asking for my help again. You hear me? No matter what you need."

Marnie was a Finder. For a fee, Marnie *acquired* things for the down and out. Sophie wasn't a stranger to her requests. If she denied them, she had a history of losing things.

"Then we're leaving." Her threat carried weight. Marnie did things her way. She tugged on Kellie's arm, but she didn't, or couldn't, move.

"Marnie...I can't...I'm staying." Kellie's sweet face twisted with determination.

"We need to get her inside." Sophie wasn't about to let Marnie's paranoia result in a disastrous situation. They weren't getting two feet without her.

"Marnie, please." Kellie laid a hand on Marnie's

arm.

"Fine, but remember I'm trusting you." Marnie moved aside and Sophie let out a breath of relief. Her capitulation didn't stop her from throwing one last insult. "Don't get stupid on me."

She knew better than to react. To retaliate. To let Marnie's words hurt her. Sophie reached into her coat pocket for her key card. They were all biding their time to get what they wanted. Right now she needed answers.

"Who's she running from? The police?" Sophie held up a hand when Marnie glared a protest. "Let's cut through the bullshit. The least you can do is give me a heads up to any potential trouble."

She did not need members of the Vancouver Police Department showing up at her clinic in the days to come and scaring away half her patients.

Nor did she need a lawsuit.

"No. No details."

Sophie swiped her card then punched in her security access code. "So, we're going with you were out for a stroll when you stumbled across a pregnant woman out in a storm. What about the father? Her family?"

"Absent. And absent." Marnie stuffed her hand into her hoodie pocket. The gun she yanked out looked very real and very deadly. "That's all you need to know. I'll do whatever I need to do to protect her. And you. All of us."

"Oh my God, Marnie! What are you doing?" Kellie reached out. Sophie stopped her hand, willed her to stay still, even though it was possible she knew this new Marnie better than Sophie knew the old one.

"Drop it. Now." Sophie held on tighter to Kellie, her heart close to stopping, or breaking. "Have you lost your mind? Put it away."

"No more questions. No outside interference." Marnie's hand shook, the gun wobbled, and Sophie tried to inch Kellie closer to the unlocked door. To the only security available. "I'll look after things."

Determination, delusion, and drug addiction didn't make a great combo. Still it was a new low. She tried to slip her hand in her pocket and reach her phone. Her heart rate doubled. She strived for calm. "Okay. Put the gun away or I don't go another step."

"I'm trusting you." Marnie choked over the words. She lowered the gun until Sophie worried she'd shoot herself in the foot. "But I'm not taking any chances. Not with her safety. Or yours."

There was only one way to deal with Marnie——head on. Again the wind picked up around them, Sophie leaned in to try and block Kellie from the worst of it while staring down Marnie. "You can't bring the gun into the clinic. I mean it, get rid of it."

She waited. Marnie glared. Kellie groaned.

"Stop being stupid and get rid of the gun. I don't move until you do." Now Sophie meant every word. And Marnie knew it. They had the same granite sense of stubbornness in common. Marnie's lip curled but she gave a slight jerk of her head.

"Dispose of it while I get her settled in the clinic." It would give her an opportunity to call for assistance away from Marnie's interference.

"No. You wait here." Marnie stuck her hand out, her expression adamant.

"Then hurry up." A shudder went through Kellie

and Sophie rubbed her arm. "I've got you. You're safe now."

Despite her assurances to the contrary, she worked on getting the door open and Kellie through it while keeping Marnie in her sights. The snow pelted down on them. By now road conditions had to suck eggs. The temperature plummeted. Their list of complications grew.

Sophie hoped it didn't come down to praying for a miracle. Marnie inched her way along the outside wall of the clinic. Sophie propped open the door. Marnie stuffed the gun down into the space between the wall and the dirty, ravaged dumpster. Sophie gritted her teeth and tried to get Kellie moving and inside.

"Come on, I've got you. You're safe now," she whispered. They were halfway in when another contraction rippled through Kellie's slim body. Sophie whispered more words of encouragement. She caught Marnie's approach out of the corner of her eye. Opportunity lost, she rubbed a hand over Kellie's back.

The echoes of Kellie's efforts ricocheted off the walls of the empty back entryway. Sophie didn't suffer from lack of confidence as a physician, but success required the proper surroundings. If the storm worsened and they lost power she'd have a disaster on her hands. Her priority was Kellie and getting her to a hospital, whether Marnie agreed or not.

****

Caleb Quinn was smart. His new letterhead, business cards, and prime parking spot proof of how hard he worked. He was ranked one of Canada's top lawyers under forty. He'd made partner at the unheard of age of thirty-two. He was charming. Ask anyone.

Women enjoyed his company. He was discreet. Generous. In bed and out of it.

He was attracted to Dr. Sophie Monroe, wanted to get to know her better. So what? Sexual attraction wasn't a crime. It was the second decade of the twenty-first century, people hooked up. He picked up a scarf, tossed it back, tuned out the most annoying Christmas song ever recorded. An over-crowded department store at closing on Christmas Eve? How much lower could he sink? Like the gift of a scarf was going to improve her opinion of him. He'd probably have more luck if he showed up with a package of tongue depressors.

Yep, he had brilliant future written all over him. Disgusted, he grabbed up the blue cashmere scarf set and headed for the endless checkout line. The cashier spotted him and beamed in his direction. He offered a polite smile and she gave him a little finger wave. Caleb reciprocated, anything to get her moving faster. People turned to stare. He ignored them and thought of the night ahead. Of Sophie.

Dinner and dancing in the decadent Four Seasons Park Ballroom. His law firm was pulling out all the stops. Safe Night's Refuge needed tonight's proceeds. He wanted to see six figures on the cheque they handed them. He met with broken families in his office every day. It was refreshing to help families struggling to stay together.

His pretty, black-haired pixie with her intelligent green eyes and quick wit would have Carson Cooper's clients throwing cash at her. Honest, engaging, and passionate, she captivated. Her smile was a hint too wide and just this side of mocking. She was an irresistible combination of temptress and warrior. Too bad her cute little nose turned up at the sight of him.

The line inched forward. A harried customer shoved past, bags in hand, on his way to the doors and freedom. Caleb checked in with the blond cashier. He sighed. Glanced at his watch. Rotated his shoulders. She scanned items, instructed customers to insert their card, bagged their items with agonizing slowness. No wonder, her fingernails were purple talons.

Not Sophie's. Hers were short and unpainted. He supposed doctors didn't do manicures. Not that she looked like any doctor he'd ever met, in her faded jeans and leather jacket. The thought of her in a dress and high heels had him reaching up to loosen his tie.

He'd set out to charm her, instead she'd challenged his ideologies. Had accused him of being in denial. Worse, biased in favor of the privileged. It had stung, and wound him up enough to challenge her to a date. She would accompany him to the Silent Night, Safe Night Gala. One night to prove their agendas weren't at odds. A chance to show he wasn't the ass she assumed he was. She'd agreed. Because she wanted to prove him wrong.

Then Tiffany had walked in and given the impression they were involved. Not true. Never would be. But office politics were his problem, not Sophie's. The atmosphere in the room had gotten a lot less friendly, but it had been too late for Sophie to back out.

So, he may or may not have a date for tonight, which meant things could get a little awkward when he arrived to pick her up.

The customer in front of him glanced over her shoulder, a questioning look on her exhausted face. Caleb realized he was talking out loud. Further proof

Sophie was already making him the kind of crazy he tried to avoid.

"Sorry." He offered a shrug and a smile. "Just going through last-minute lists in my head."

With a no-comment kind of eye roll, she turned to face the front of the line and the cashier who was taking a timeout to check her phone. He glanced at his watch again. They weren't due at the fundraiser for an hour and a half. Plenty of time. His pocket vibrated. He pulled out his cell phone.

Sophie calling.

He put his phone to his ear. "Sophie?"

"I'm sorry. An emergency at the clinic has come up. I have to cancel tonight."

"Cancel? You can't cancel." She had to be kidding. Didn't she? "500 people are expecting us for dinner."

"It can't be helped. Please give everyone my apologies. I have no choice. I have to deal with this. There's no one else." She sounded distracted, and although he didn't know her well, worried. She rushed through the words so fast Caleb scrambled to keep up. Someone yelled in the background. "Look, I have to go. I'm going to text you the number of Amanda Brine. She runs Safe Night. She's filling in for me."

"Wait a minute. You can't blow this off. People are counting on you." He was counting on her.

"Caleb. If there was any other way to handle this situation, I'd take it. Believe me…emergency…help." A muffled clanking noise masked most of her words.

He strained to listen. Gave up. "I can't hear you."

More noise in the background. "…to go."

Dial tone.

"Unbelievable. Shit." This time the woman in front

of him turned to glare. He held up his phone, tried for sheepish and sorry. He was neither. "Sorry. Bad connection."

What the hell? This evening meant everything to Sophie and Safe Night's Refuge. The size of the donations depended on her wooing some very important, insanely wealthy people. After dinner the evening was spent garnering further support and hitting up the who's who of Vancouver for donations. She wouldn't shrug off the loss of funds. Something was wrong. He didn't know how he knew it but he did. He hit redial and listened to her phone ring and ring and ring. His decision was no decision at all. There was enough time left to check things out. He rushed toward the big glass doors. The pull on his arm stopped him in his tracks.

"You plan on paying for that, pal?" The skinny pimped out security guard regarded him with zeal in his eye, one hand flexing over his portable radio.

"Excuse me?"

The guard shot a pointed look at his hands.

"This? Changed my mind. Not her style." He shoved the scarf still clutched in his hand at the scowling mall cop and hustled through the huge doors and into the worst snowstorm Vancouver had suffered through in decades.

Back at his office he spared a few minutes for damage control. He filled the other partners in before contacting the Executive Director of Safe Nights. By the time he pulled his Range Rover out of his private parking spot the streets were next to impassable.

The half hour drive to Sophie's downtown clinic took him two hours. He slid his way into the all but deserted parking lot next to a vehicle buried in snow. To celebrate his safe arrival he lowered his throbbing head to the steering wheel and closed his eyes. His hands still welded to the wheel. There was no way either of them were getting back to the Four Seasons in time for anything.

Outside the Rover the waves of shifting snow appeared undisturbed. His shoe clad feet disappeared in a freezing bank of snow. Wonderful. He tugged the collar of his overcoat closer. Chances were the good doctor was going to be pissed to see him here. But he'd learned the hard way to trust his instincts.

The front door was secured but he hit pay dirt at the backdoor. It was unlocked, which worried him. The odor of disinfectant assaulted his nose. He paused. Lights on up ahead suggested activity. A hoarse cry stopped him in his tracks then sent him rushing forward.

"Sophie." He reached a bank of closed doors. Another cry pierced the air. "Sophie. Are you all right? It's Caleb."

The second door from the end flung open. A woman charged out. Sophie pushed past her into the hallway.

"Caleb." Confusion replaced disbelief. Her amazing green eyes narrowed. "What are you doing here?"

A low groan filled the room behind her and Sophie disappeared again. Caleb's view was blocked by the mystery woman. Her dark hair hung in strings around her weathered face. She pushed the strands back behind her ears. Wrinkles fanned out from narrowed, staring eyes. The stench of body order and stale cigarettes filled the air. She barely reached his shoulder yet she had the upper hand. They both knew it.

Then Sophie was at the door again. "Marnie, it's okay, he's with me."

"You told someone we were here?" demanded the older woman.

Sophie scrubbed a hand over her face. "No. Of course not."

"Then what's he doing here?" Marnie stabbed a finger in his direction.

Sophie's tone was guarded. "I'm supposed to be at a fundraiser. Caleb is sort of my date."

Marnie curled her lip and subjected him to a full body scan. "You have a date? With him?"

Caleb inhaled, slow and silent. He let her sarcasm slide. In his line of work keeping your head was part of the job description. "I came to check on Sophie."

The exhaustion cleared from Sophie's eyes. "Excuse me?"

Caleb backtracked. "Okay, not the best choice of words, but—"

"Is this guy for real?" demanded Marnie.

Sophie rolled her eyes. "Unfortunately, yes."

"I don't like him. Get rid of him." The older woman crossed her arms and gave her best impression of a brick wall.

"Charming." To Sophie, he asked, "Can I have a moment?"

"Marnie, relax." Sophie stepped around her. Marnie flinched but didn't budge. "I need you back in the room with Kellie while I speak to Caleb."

It worked for him. He wasn't going anywhere until Sophie explained what was going on. He waited until her eyes were back on him. "Are you okay?"

"Why don't you go to hell?" Marnie pushed forward. Sophie put an arm out to block her path. Caleb tensed, ready to defend Sophie. Or himself.

"Sophie, I need an answer. Now." He inched forward.

"I'm fine." She put out a hand to ward him off. "Just kind of in the middle of something right now."

He moved closer until the tips of her fingers pressed against his chest. "You're sure everything's all right? It doesn't look all right to me."

"Why don't you back the fuck up, buddy?" Marnie fought to push past Sophie's arm.

Caleb met her glare for glare. "Someone better tell me what the hell is going on before I call the cops."

"That's enough. Both of you." Her voice lowered. "Keep it down."

"Then start explaining." He was past caring it was a demand he had no right to make.

Sophie turned to Marnie. "Marnie stay with Kellie. I'm going to talk with Caleb."

"No cops." Her demand hung in the air. She shoved her hands under her armpits and rocked on the balls of her feet.

"No cops." Sophie took a step back, her tongue did a quick swipe over her lower lip. "But you have to know I've called for an ambulance and—"

"What?" Marnie's scarred face twisted. "I trusted you."

Sophie's chin went up. "You brought her to me. She's my patient. It's my call."

"You had no right—"

"I had every right." Sophie shoved a hand through

her short, dark hair. "Anyway, it's irrelevant. According to the dispatcher, it'll be hours before they can get here. There's a storm outside, remember?"

Caleb didn't want to add to the bad news but he had no choice. "It's a mess across the city. Accidents everywhere. Marine Drive is closed. So is the Trans-Canada Highway at Memorial Bridge. Huge accident. Lots of smaller ones. The authorities are asking people to stay home."

"So, right now I need you to go sit with Kellie while I talk to Caleb."

As soon as the door shut behind Marnie, Sophie leaned back against it and brushed a hand across her forehead. "You practice family law, right?"

"Right." Not sure where she was going with it, Caleb nodded at the unexpected question. "Why?"

"I have a patient in labor. I've only managed to get a bit of her story. But…it seems she's on the run and terrified of the father finding her. Marnie is frantic I don't call anybody. I don't know what's going on, other than its messy. And I'll be honest. I'm worried. We're trapped here." She shook her head, her beautiful eyes showing signs of fatigue. His fingers clench into fists.

"You think he's violent. Is there a chance he'll show up here?" All the protective instincts he possessed snapped at their leash. The junkyard dog compulsion so extreme his vision blurred.

"I doubt it." Sophie's lip curled. "Getting his hands dirty isn't his style. Then again…"

"If he's a problem, I need a name." He tried to focus. This was crazy. He didn't know what to do with the adrenaline dump. Except pull her close, then drag her out of here. To protect and def—

"Jason Drummond." Sophie's head bobbed in reaction to his slack-jawed disbelief. Her eyes wide with understanding. "I wish I were kidding. But she's insisting Prince Charming and the heir apparent to all those lovely shopping malls and luxury hotels is the father of her baby."

Now she had his attention in a whole different way.

"No." Caleb shook his head. Not possible. The idea was ludicrous. "No way."

Sophie grimaced at him. "Please tell me he's not one of your country club buddies."

Close enough, they belonged to the same gym, were friends of a sort, not information he cared to share at the moment. He hedged. "We know each other."

"Oh, Caleb." She looked straight at him, disappointment taking the lush out of her generous mouth. "Tell me if this is going to be a conflict of interest for you? If it is, you have to leave. Now."

"It's not." No way in hell he was leaving her to deal with this situation all alone. He sidetracked her. "Who's the other woman? Marnie? How's she involved?"

"Marnie is…" She looked away and back again. "It's complicated."

Brilliant, neither of them was sharing the whole story. Caleb put her omission aside for now. He wanted a straight answer to his next question. "Is she dangerous?"

"Yesterday I would have said no. But earlier she pulled out a gun. She's desperate. More so than usual. I can't say for sure."

Maybe he'd heard wrong, because what the—

Caleb commandeered her arm and pulled her

further down the hall. "Pardon me? Are you saying she's armed?"

She tried to shake him off but he held on. "Not anymore. I made her leave the gun outside."

His hand tightened as his heart rate spiked. "Has she left the room?"

Sophie's other hand went to her throat. She thought back. "I sent her for some water from the kitchen but I'm pretty sure she went there and came straight back." She nodded, reassured. "No, she wasn't gone long and there was no evidence she'd been out in the snow. Besides, if she had a gun she would have shot you already."

"Good to know." Because she was serious. She hadn't said it to amuse or belittle. Caleb forced himself to think back to the parking lot and the undisturbed snow. His footprints had been the only ones out there. "Okay, tell me where she left it and I'll go and lock it in my car."

Explaining the details made her sad. It was in her pretty green eyes, the stoop of her shoulders. How she looked away and didn't look back.

"I'll take care of it." Unable to resist his hand trailed over the rising phoenix inked into her forearm. Strong and soft.

"I need to get back in there." She pulled away and his hand dropped. Worry clouded her eyes. She nibbled on her bottom lip. "I need to ask you another favor. It's huge."

"Anything." He cringed on the inside. He didn't make vague promises. He was careful to keep it simple. Always. The dim light of the hallway and the sweat of trauma must have fogged his brain.

"Marnie's very close to Kellie. I've never seen her develop this close an attachment to anyone. I can't rely on her to do what I need her to do if things go south. I need someone in there who can assist me with *whatever* comes up. I need someone who can contain Marnie if I'm forced to do something she doesn't agree with. I need you in there, Caleb. In case something goes wrong."

He was pretty sure he could handle Marnie the Ballbuster. But assisting with a birth wasn't on his bucket list. This is what came of making reckless promises. Moot point. He wasn't letting her go in there alone. Not with someone who might or might not be dangerous.

He nodded his answer. "But you have a Plan B for if something goes wrong? Medically? Right?"

"You are my Plan B, Caleb." She smiled, patted him on the cheek. He stared down at her and Sophie laughed as she backed up toward the treatment room door. "Now, aren't you glad you came to 'check on me'?"

Nice. Now she makes jokes. Good to know she had a sense of humor buried under all those ideas on how to change the world.

"Here's hoping we don't need to implement Plan B." He tagged along after her retreating back, not daring to breathe until she was back inside and the door closed in his face. Then he remembered it was something he needed to do to remain upright. Deep breaths. Deep. Slow. Calm. Or he'd end up passing out in the hallway.

Babies were born every day. Women had been birthing babies since the beginning of time. Babies came out. Out places he didn't want to think about in that context. Ever. But they did come out. Eventually. Didn't they?

Caleb headed for the backdoor his flight response activated and sending out a high alert. It spread from his gut to his extremities causing them to bunch and flex with the need to hit the road running.

He didn't know anything about delivering babies. Or how to wrap his head around the allegation Jason was the father. He knew the man. They'd gone to school together. They moved in the same circles. His wife was a dear friend. In seven days, at their annual New Year's Eve bash, Jason was expected to announce his intention to run for mayor of Vancouver.

A blast of cold air blew snow in his face when he pushed the back door open. The sharp slap of winter woke him up. Bizarre accusations and the future of municipal politics could wait. One problem at a time. He had to help deliver a baby. In the Low Track. On Christmas Eve. In a small, rundown, last chance kind of place clinic. Because there was no way to get to the overcrowded hospital.

Cue the angels.

He grabbed some gloves out of his vehicle and left the engine running. He shuffled back through the snow to search for Marnie's gun. The battered dumpster stood guard against the clinic wall, and what a wall it was. He stared, amazed. In the light cast from the street and his headlights, he studied the mural. It was spray painted by an artist who knew his stuff. A slow spinning earth hovered over winged hands. He moved closer, ran a hand over rough brick. Items flew from the globe into the atmosphere. The detail was incredible.

It made stalling a pleasure but wasn't going to get him anywhere. He pushed back his hair and got to work. It didn't take long to dig the handgun out of its hiding place. It was right where Sophie said. He wrapped his frozen, stiff fingers around the handle. Tested the weight then held it way out in front of him confident no one was watching his sissy act from the shadows of the blizzard. He didn't know anything about guns and he wasn't looking to change his lack any time soon. It could be loaded or not. He had no idea how to check and no desire to shoot himself in the foot.

Back inside his vehicle he opened the glove compartment and stuffed the gun inside, locked it. He pulled his hands out of stiff wet gloves made more for driving than warmth and rubbed some heat into them. Then he offered up a prayer. It was a night for miracles, after all. Baby miracles to boot.

Please, please, please no complications. Or blood. Amen.

He and the sight of blood did not mix. Bad things happened. Embarrassing things. He scrubbed a hand over his face. No passing out. No tossing his cookies in front of the womenfolk. He inhaled, blew out a breath. Game on.

Caleb skidded his way back toward the clinic. Wet snow clung to his clothes, his hair, it filled his shoes. He ignored the discomfort, pulled out his cellphone and flipped through his contacts until he came to the name he wanted. Jason Drummond's number flashed up on the screen. He stared at it, thumb hovering over the call button. It couldn't be true. Jason Drummond? The man was far from stupid. Or careless. Savvy when it came to the public and its opinions. With a care for being seen in the best light. In the last decade he'd gone from playboy heir to corporate development kingpin. But before that had come high school.

Boarding school, to be exact. There'd been a girl then too. Scholarship recipient Kimberley McKay hadn't come from the usual moneyed background. She'd struggled to fit in, Caleb one of her few friends. Then she'd started dating Jason Drummond and everything had changed. She'd relished the perks. For a time. Two months in she'd come to him in a panic with a wild story about Jason drugging her. She'd asked for his help. Caleb had gone to Jason, asked him questions. He'd laughed it off, said he was the one who'd broken things off. She was upset, more than that she was unstable. He hinted at major mental health issues. Two days later she'd quit school in the middle of final exams and moved across the country with her parents. He'd never heard from her again.

His guilt at not keeping in touch had evaporated over the years, but he'd never forgotten. He paused, one hand clutched around the frozen door handle. Once he walked through the door there was no going back. He was all the way in. He'd either discover Marnie and her friend were lying or telling the truth. Easy enough to deal with the deception. The truth was a whole different matter. Bringing it to light meant challenging one of the most powerful men in Vancouver. If Jason Drummond had fathered a baby out of wedlock? A family empire built on the shaky stilts of strident conservative values was in danger of sinking into a swamp of scandal.

Turn around and he was all the way out. It was his choice. But not an option. He shoved his phone back in his pocket and pulled open the door.

Chapter Two

Caleb made his way down the hallway taking in all the details in an effort to drag it out. No anemic prints or watery vistas on these walls, but a litter of paper announcing the place and times for AA meetings, posters announcing a memorial march, free meals, and so on. And photographs. Hundreds of them: men, women, and children. Stapled to bulletin boards dedicated to "Have you seen…" Or "Last Seen…" scenarios.

Caleb searched the faces knowing he'd recognize no one. The hard worn expressions of the lost didn't match the gloss and polish of his crowd. They didn't travel in the same circles. For the first time in his life, facing this forest of lost souls and loved ones desperate to find them, he wasn't sure it was a good thing.

He knocked on the treatment room door still eyeing pictures of the missing trying to commit some to memory. The people he knew didn't disappear. They let you know exactly where they were, who they were with, and why you should care.

Sophie opened the door and moved back to let him in. Her expression did nothing to reassure. Eyes alert, mouth set, chin raised, she signaled a call to arms. He had nothing to bring to the situation except an aversion to blood. One foot in the door and his heart rate spiked. The woman on the narrow makeshift bed shuddered.

Her moan made Caleb's hair stand on end. He couldn't resist asking if everything was okay.

Marnie focused in on him from her guard dog position beside her. Her scarred face shiny with perspiration. "You'd be screaming too. If you were getting ready to push a watermelon out of a hole the size of a walnut."

He forced his rigid facial muscles to relax into a smile. "No doubt about it."

She didn't give an inch. "He shouldn't be here."

Sophie sighed. There were circles under her eyes. She dabbed her wrist across her forehead and Caleb's chest tightened. She was worn out. "Well, he is. So, deal with it."

"Does anyone object to me knowing who our patient is?" Knowing full well someone would.

"None of your business," Marnie offered. "If you're going to be in here, stand there and shut the fuck up."

"None of us are going anywhere, so we might as well allow introductions." Sophie put a gentle hand on her patient's forehead and brushed a piece of her hair to the side of her face. "This is Kellie Andrews. Kellie, this is Caleb Quinn. He's a friend and he's here to help."

Kellie lifted a tired hand, let it drop. Caleb tried to hide his shock at her age. Barely out of her teens, dirty and haggard, she wasn't someone Jason would look twice at, let alone notice.

Marnie snorted as she reached into her pocket. Caleb braced but all she pulled out was a battered pack of cigarettes.

Sophie pointed to the pack of smokes. "Put them

away or get out. Take your pick."

The cigarette crumbled apart when Marnie jabbed it back into the worn case. "I'm not going anywhere."

That made two of them.

"I'm staying." He owed it to Sophie and to Jason.

The woman on the bed moaned. "Oh God, here comes another one."

Sophie pointed at both of them. "Fine. Everyone's staying?"

Caleb faced off against Marnie. It was obvious Marnie was protecting the woman on the bed and he wasn't leaving without the woman in the polar bear print scrubs. Stalemate.

Sophie shot him a look. He nodded.

She reciprocated with a brace-yourself look. "Okay then. Make yourself useful."

He shrugged out of his suit jacket and tossed it over a chair, same with his tie. In the process of rolling up his sleeves he made eye contact with Marnie. Her snarl contorted her scar and it brutalized her face. The effect was chilling. She knew it. A slow smile eased the ugliness but not her meaning.

Careful.

Caleb raised a brow and prepared to face off against a woman who'd seen her share of battles. Too skinny for her small frame, her clothes ragged and filthy, she was a poster child for the down and out. It also made her an unlikely candidate for white knight.

"Marnie. Over here."

"Coming." Marnie shifted her position never taking her eyes of Caleb. Somehow Kellie survived the contraction. He didn't know how. Tension, compounded by a bout of nausea, had sweat pooling in places he'd rather not mention. Then there was a lull and Kellie closed her eyes.

"So, does someone want to fill me in on what's going on?" Going on the offensive might get him some answers, and it beat staring at the unknown girl on the table. Scared, not to mention in pain, she looked too frail to deliver a letter let alone a baby.

"I don't know, has hell frozen over?"

"I'm here." He spread his hands hoping for conciliatory. "I want to help."

"The question is why?" Marnie shot an accusing glare in Sophie's direction.

"I get you don't trust me and why should you? But give me a chance. I could be more help than you realize." With whatever this was.

"Marnie, relax." Kellie sounded worn out, and no wonder, he was exhausted and all he was doing was standing there. "It's okay. I don't mind."

"Well, golly gee, let's all pull up chairs and spill our guts to the new guy. I'll start. Hello, my name's Marnie and my private life is none of your business."

"Marnie." It was a warning and came from Sophie.

Caleb spread out his hands. "Just offering a little goodwill."

"Yeah, well, you don't look like the goodwill type to me."

"I don't think we want to go down the who-looks-like-what road."

"What? Not pretty enough for you?" Marnie blew him a kiss before grasping Kellie's hand.

"You want me to think you're pretty?" Caleb countered.

Marnie sneered. "A liberal elitist like you? I don't

think so."

"Enough. This isn't about either of you." Sophie gestured at Marnie before nodding at Caleb. "I hope you're ready for this Caleb because it's going to be a rough one."

Sophie bent and whispered in Kellie's ear. Her face twisted in pain. Ready or not, he wasn't leaving. He offered up a silent prayer, planted his feet, and stripped his face of expression. "Where do you want me?"

Sophie pointed. "Stay where you are. An examination table makes for a narrow bed. We need help keeping her on it. To keep things stable."

He braced for the worst.

An anguished cry left the woman on the bed. She grabbed Marnie's hand. He knew by her grimace how much pressure Kellie was exerting. Marnie's eyes started to water. He wanted to grin, but he was too damned freaked out.

"Caleb." He forced his attention back to Sophie. "Make sure she doesn't get too far over to that side."

Right. Falling off the bed would be bad. His hands shook as he tried to figure out where to place them. They hovered in the air like he was practicing some kind of exorcism. He still hadn't decided where to position them when Sophie rounded the table and put them in place for him.

"It hurts." Kellie tried to curl up against the pain. There was nothing Caleb could do about his flinch. Kellie gasped before her worried expression sought out Sophie. "Is it supposed to hurt this much? What if something's wrong?"

"Everything's fine," answered Sophie. He didn't know where she put all the passion and heat she brought to her fundraising. Here, under pressure, calm surrounded her and confidence seeped out of every pour. "As long as the baby keeps moving down a little further each time you're doing fine."

Forty minutes later Sophie sent him to the supply cabinet with a list as long as his arm. Marnie looked ready to volunteer to go instead so he beat tracks for the door and a little fresh air. Thanks to the symbiotic ingenuity of sweat, fear, and pain the room was stifling hot. He took his time. Not putting any thought into why she might need a suture kit. Nope, he wasn't going there. When he walked back into the room it didn't appear much had changed.

"Not long now." Sophie looked over at him. He figured her reassurance was more for Kellie's benefit than his. It didn't stop him from praying she was right. And he wasn't having kids. Ever. No way was he putting anybody he loved through this kind of torture.

"What can I do?" He needed to keep his mind busy. He stacked his packages on the little desk space there was left. Once again he was left wondering what to do with his hands, or the sick feeling in his stomach.

"Keep doing what you're doing. Kellie, don't forget to breathe. I'm going to get you to push on the count of three. Ready?"

Kellie nodded. Like an idiot, so did he.

"One. Two. Three. Push."

Caleb figured the ideal position for him was by Kellie's head and as far from the birthing canal as it was possible to get. He didn't know where Kellie found the strength to do it, but she did. She pushed. And she kept on the relentless pattern of pushing and taking a short break for another godforsaken hour. It was clear

Sophie was in her element. She kept them focused. Comforted Kellie. Issued orders. He couldn't help but respond to her confidence, her command of the situation. It was loud, messy, and tense, but she never lost her cool. If he weren't so preoccupied with avoiding the sight of things he'd rather never witness, he might have found it a total turn on.

"Okay, one more push should do it." And she was right. Thank you, God.

A baby emerged into Sophie's waiting hands covered in gunk. Also red-faced and screaming. Then it was time to cut the cord. She wasn't going to use—his knees wobbled and the world went blurry. He heard his name over the flush of sweat.

"Marnie, shove a chair under him. Quick."

Something solid hit him in the back of the knees. "Put your big girl panties on, for fuck sake."

He sat.

And remained seated by sheer force of will, his hands fused to the sides of the chair. Thankfully the darkness started to fade. A little light appeared around the edges, then color. Shapes. Reality. Marnie glaring at him, hands on hips. She yanked out her pack of cigs, remembered and shoved the crumpled pack back. She wasn't happy. As in give-me-a-minute-to-go-get-my-gun unhappy.

Caleb ignored her and concentrated on Sophie, who was busy with the baby. Bad idea. But she was quick about it, and he supposed all the slime needed to come off somehow. He caught a glimpse of male parts. She handed the baby boy over to his mother. The three women congratulated each other. Transformed from soldiers to gooey chocolate centers in the blink of an eye. He didn't know how they did it. He needed a bottle of scotch and a therapist's couch. Stat.

His presence wasn't required for…whatever came next. He escaped the room to sag against a wall in the hallway. The slide down to the floor was a relief. His watch registered 10:30 pm. It felt like an eternity had passed. His head fell back against the wall and he shut his eyes. Jeezus God, they'd delivered a baby. Sophie, even Marnie, more than him, but still he'd witnessed a birth. No causalities, except maybe him. He'd had his doubts a couple of times, but they'd done it. Well, Kellie had done all the work.

Was he a Drummond baby? An heir to the heir of a real estate dynasty? She had to be lying. Jason wasn't the type to cheat on his wife. He was devoted to her. Loving her aside, his reputation meant everything to him. He was angling for the top job at city hall. He wouldn't jeopardize his chance of being the youngest mayor in the history of any Canadian city for a young girl barely out of high school.

Why claim a connection when all it took was a DNA test to prove otherwise? His eyes stayed shut when the door opened and closed. Someone joined him on the floor. He resisted the urge to cover his balls in case it was Marnie. It wasn't. No amount of antiseptic and sweat could drown out the underlying scent of Sophie.

He opened his eyes. "How are mother and baby?"

"Doing fine."

"You were brilliant in there." He smiled, looked at her, lost a little piece of his heart. "I want you to know, if I'm ever stuck in another freak snowstorm with a woman giving birth I want you by my side."

"Well, kudos to you as well. You didn't do too bad yourself. Until the end. But Kellie did the hard work. All the credit goes to her."

"Understood. In my own defense, it did get kind of disgusting there at the finish."

"Duly noted."

"Why do women do it?"

She rolled her lovely green eyes. "You know the whole stork thing is a myth right?"

"Too bad." And he meant it.

"Yeah, well, she's got some pretty big obstacles to overcome yet." Her words carried the dull weight of concern. "She's very young. Her only support being Marnie, which is scary as hell. And now she's responsible for another human being."

"Did you find out anything else about her? How old is she?"

She sighed. "I didn't get much, but I do know she's eighteen."

"Shit." He stared at the cluttered wall and sea of paper faces across from him. "Do you think she's telling the truth?"

"About Jason Drummond being the father?" She frowned. "Easy enough to prove or disprove. And Marnie might be a lot of things. Delusional. Paranoid. Even a liar when it serves her purpose, but…I don't know. I'm getting a bad feeling."

"I know Jason." *Sort of.* "Have for years. And the things they're saying? I'm having a very hard time believing."

Wasn't he?

Sophie shrugged. "All it takes is a DNA test."

"Or the threat of having to provide it." The final

outcome didn't matter. The hint of scandal alone was enough to ruin Jason's plans. "He's planning on running for mayor. If you wanted to strike out at him, or get something from him, the timing's perfect."

"Then they went to a lot of trouble to arrange a pregnancy. And she's doesn't appear to have been living in the lap of luxury."

"Exactly. Motive."

"Are you thinking like a lawyer or a friend?"

"Maybe a bit of both."

"Do me a favor? Wait until you hear the whole story." She braced her hands on her knees. "I should get back in there. Check on them. Who knows when the ambulance will get here. I contacted them again, let them know it wasn't an emergency. They'll be here as soon as they can. Probably another couple of hours."

Before he had a chance to respond the treatment room door opened and Marnie looked out. "Kellie wants to talk to the lawyer."

He ignored the contempt in her voice and pushed to his feet. This was one of those moments. The defining kind. He knew it down to the soles of his feet. There was a public relations mess on the other side of the door. Not only for Jason Drummond. If Kellie was telling the truth about paternity, the people involved in exposing it were going to get hit with the same shit storm. It was going to come hard. And fast. The Drummonds' weren't known for their clemency.

It couldn't matter. "Lead the way."

Sophie put a hand on his arm. "Be careful with her. She's tired and she's exhausted."

"Cut me some slack, okay?" He traced a finger down the side of her cheek. Her look of confusion

33

reassured him. Good to know she didn't have all the answers. "Or did you miss the part where I said I was good at my job?"

Her eyes shifted away from his. "Then let's get this done."

With a finger to her chin he drew her look back to him. "But you have to know that child in there is my first priority. Along with the truth. If I find out she's lying, or in any way incapable…"

"I know." Her deep breath matched his own.

But he'd keep an open mind, reserve judgment until he heard her story. He didn't shy away from hard decisions. Neither did he make them lightly. No matter the cost. Not when a child's welfare was at stake.

****

Kellie sniffed into a tissue. Caleb was no stranger to tears. His mother shed her share, both honest and calculating. Clients shed them in his office. He'd shed a few when the Canucks had lost the Stanley Cup. He didn't let her tears influence him.

But some admiration crept in when she set her narrow shoulders back. At her awkward attempts with her baby. When she found her groove and smiled down at the squirming bundle in her arms.

Damn it, he didn't want to like her.

"You wanted to talk to me?" He pulled over the only chair in the room and motioned to Sophie. "You're exhausted. Sit."

Sophie proved he was right by sitting down without argument. But she shifted the chair closer to Kellie. When she looked up at him her eyes were full of warning.

"I'll stand, thanks for asking." Marnie crossed her

arms over her skinny chest obscuring the big red Nike swoosh.

"I wasn't, but good to know." He caught the tail end of Sophie's eye roll. He stifled a smirk and turned to Kellie. "Are you sure you're up for this? We can always do this in a couple of days, when you're rested, had a chance to organize your thoughts."

"I've done nothing but think for two months." She shifted on the bed. "No, I'll feel better once I tell you."

"Don't worry. We're not here to pass judgment." Sophie reached over and smoothed a hand over the baby's head. "Take all the time you need."

"I need...legal advice." Her words faded in and out. Caleb shifted closer to catch them. "You don't have to help me if you don't want to, but...ah...I wanted you to hear my side of the story so you could decide."

Caleb didn't need to hear it to know Kellie Andrews was in over her head. The Drummonds were generous when inspired by tax breaks. If it garnered the right kind of press. They wouldn't gift the steam off their piss to a homeless teenage mother from the Downtown Eastside. It wasn't a secret. They'd rode the hard love, up by your boot straps angle all the way to the top of the Fortune 500 pile.

"Anything you need." Sophie rubbed a hand up and down Kellie's arm.

Not so fast. "How about we strike a deal? You be honest with us, we'll be honest with you."

Sophie shot him a look fuelled by exasperation. Too bad.

"Thank you," whispered Kellie. She laid a cheek against her baby's head. Whether the move was choreographed or not, it pulled at him.

Marnie cleared her throat. Without turning her head Kellie's eyes sought her out, her look questioning. Marnie nodded once.

Caleb didn't like it. Something was off. Instinct warned him to take care. To proceed with caution. As young and innocent as Kellie seemed, she wasn't in this alone. She checked in with Marnie every few seconds. She waited for her signals. No doubt about it. Marnie was in charge of this show. But what did she have to gain?

Kellie glanced at Caleb, caught him studying her. Her head dipped and she froze. Marnie rescued her. "She doesn't have any money to pay for a lawyer."

"I do pro bono work for an organization called Legal Tree. They have an office a few blocks from here." His time amounted to a few hours every couple of weeks. It wasn't something he broadcasted to the public. He focused all his attention on Kellie even though Sophie turned to stare at him. He pulled out a smile guaranteed to charm. "If we proceed, I don't see why this can't fall under the work I do for them."

Kellie sagged in relief, offered him a shy thanks. It lifted some of the sadness out of the room. The tension in him eased.

Marnie rolled her eyes. "Can we get on with this?"

They settled in to listen but Kellie stalled, reluctant or unsure of how to start.

"The best place to start is the beginning. Tell me what you want to happen." He kept his voice level, his tone even. Nothing about his demeanor suggested careers hung in the balance, friendships, a child's wellbeing.

Kellie shifted the sleepy-eyed baby in her arms. Her smile hesitant, confused, but when she cuddled her baby close the love in her eyes wasn't feigned. When she lifted her head neither was the fear. "You're not going to believe me."

"Give me a try." He didn't make any sudden movements. Didn't want to spook her. He gritted his teeth when Marnie nodded her consent.

"I worked for him. Mr. Drummond. Or his company, I guess. I came in a couple of times a week to do some temp work. He...he noticed me." She stumbled over words, teared up. Caleb stifled his frustration at her choreographed speech. Then once again it circled around to the older woman guiding her forward with another nod of her head. Kellie cleared her throat. "Things happened, we hooked up. When I realized I was pregnant I went to him. Told him. He gave me cash and told me to get an abortion. Said there'd be more money after I'd had the procedure."

Caleb frowned. "Obviously, you didn't go through with it."

"No." She shook her head, once again looking to Marnie before lowering her head and whispering, "I...I didn't."

"And you lied and told him you went through with it?" Sophie directed her question at Kellie but she watched Marnie too. Nothing obvious, covert glimpses only.

Still looking down, Kellie shook her head. "No, I never went back. He was really angry when I told him. He called me stupid. And worse. No way was I going back there."

"When you say 'things happened' what do you

mean? What kind of relationship did you have?"

"Need it spelled out for you?" Marnie taunted.

"Something like that." He refused to be baited. "Was it one night? An affair?"

"No." Kellie paused to chew on her bottom lip. She tried to shift her position, but the narrow bed made it impossible. Sophie stepped in to help her. When she was settled, Kellie picked up where she'd left off, choosing to stare at the far wall this time. "We met in his office. Got to know one another. Afterwards we met at an apartment he keeps in Chinatown."

Caleb sent a sideways glance in Sophie's direction to gauge her reaction to what Kellie was saying. It had been a while since he'd had much to do with teenage girls, but this sounded like one cold and impersonal affair. Didn't they want hearts and flowers? Justin Bieber lyrics? The narrowing of Sophie's eyes followed by the slight tilt of her head confirmed he wasn't imagining things.

"How long did this go on for?" he asked.

"Not long." Kellie shrugged. "A couple of months."

"Did you know he was married?"

She nodded. "Yes."

Okay, not a total shock, but still. "And it didn't bother you?"

"I needed the job." For the first time she looked him full in the eye, unblinking, unwavering, unapologetic.

He didn't know what to swallow first: the shock or the disbelief. "Did he threaten to fire you if you refused to sleep with him?"

"No. Nothing like that, but he never does. He loses

interest and moves on. If we keep our mouths shut we get a few bucks, well more than a few."

The sick slow glide of revulsion overran the first quick seconds of shock. He'd meant fired from her temp work job. Not…Caleb stilled. "Are you saying he paid…" He cleared his throat. "That he's done this before, with other women?"

Marnie snorted. "If by women you mean girls, then yes. The only requirement is youth. They have to be eighteen. The younger looking the better. Pretty. And he prefers them desperate or destitute, so he shops the Downtown Eastside. It's how he gets his rocks off. And good publicity to boot—employing the unemployable. His Fresh Beginnings Program sound familiar?" Her forehead shone with perspiration. She wiped it away with a shaking hand.

Caleb kept his mouth shut and shoved his fists into his front pockets. A public relations mess? If it was true it was a whole lot darker and dirtier.

"Starting to read between the lines yet, Counselor?" Her agitation picked up. "Your friend likes them young, but this is how he keeps it legal. He brings in temps. He picks one, he screws them in style, he pays them well for the privilege, and when it's over they still have a job. Of course, it's a different job far, far away from him and his precious reputation. Maybe in Calgary or a place like Toronto."

"Marnie, calm down." Sophie stepped in. Kellie fought back tears, which woke the baby who whimpered out a warning. Sophie reached for a tissue, handed it to Kellie. Then she reached for Marnie who backed up, tripping over her own feet to get away. Sophie froze.

Caleb wanted to throw up. Like Lot's wife, he couldn't resist the urge to flash a look back. To Kimberley, her outrageous accusations. The hardening started in his gut, calcifying his organs. Until his thoughts were heavy as stone. He fought to focus on the truth. Details could be manufactured. But it was her certainty, the fanatical crush of it that put him on the defensive. "I'm supposed to take your word for it?"

"That must be some world you live in? Where honesty doesn't count for shit?" Marnie's words sliced through air contaminated by the humiliation of confession.

Before he thought the motion through Caleb crowded into her personal space, put a toe over the line of his own private rules of confrontation. He spoke without weighing the consequences. "It's been a long night. I've had it with your assumptions and your attitude. You don't know jack about me, lady. So back off."

"You think I'm lying?" She spit out a laugh. "I could make you a fucking list. This time he's left a kid behind to prove it. Go ahead. Ask her how he plans on dealing with a child."

"Okay, everyone back to their corners." Sophie pushed her way between them. She put one hand on his chest, her eyes pleading.

"It's true," Kellie whispered from her makeshift hospital bed. Half cooing and half sobbing, clutching her baby to her chest. "All of what she says. I need to know how to protect my baby."

Caleb closed his eyes. He was supposed to be at a party drinking wine, eating off china plates, and impressing Sophie. Instead, he was here. He was tired.

Angry. Sickened.

And forced to ask a question he didn't want an answer to, "Has he threatened you or his child?"

"He saw me. A couple of months ago. He was with his wife." Kellie's eyes filled with more tears. For the first time her voice was harsh. "They were slumming it at a charity event at the Carnegie Centre. Lots of cameras. Lots of press. I was working the event. Part of the wait staff."

"Did he approach you?"

"No." Kellie shook her head. "I stayed as far away from them as I could for the rest of the night."

"But he contacted you after the event?"

"Yeah, he sent two guys to our apartment. They handed me an envelope and told me to leave Vancouver behind. Said if I spread lies about Jason Drummond bad things would happen."

"You said 'our apartment.' Who do you live with?"

"I was renting with another girl." Again she checked in with Marnie before proceeding. "Um, we went to school together."

"What was in the envelope?"

"An eviction notice."

Caleb's hands tightened into fists. "What happened next?"

"A week later I got fired from my other part-time job. No reason. My boss just told me to leave and not come back."

"Did you call the police after the break-in?"

Marnie's laugh boomeranged around the room her target Caleb. "Seriously? Is this guy for real?"

Kellie took pity on him. Her sad smile suggested he was too naïve for this little group, this place. Unlike the other three people in the room who had what it took to survive in a place like the Downtown Eastside. "No. They made it pretty clear talking to the cops would be a bad idea."

"But you stayed." If this was an act it was pretty damn good. So good, it was impossible to doubt her. "Why?"

"I'm not brave or anything. Or stupid either, no matter how it looks. I don't have anywhere else to go. And no money to get there if I did."

"But you said Jason gave you money." She looked away, swallowed. Caleb recognized guilt when he saw it. "How much money did he give you?"

Still avoiding eye contact she whispered, "$20,000."

Next to nothing for Jason. Hell, it was the amount Caleb had pledged to Safe Night's Refuge. His portfolio wouldn't even miss it. In fact, it was a tax break. But a king's ransom to her. And yet she'd burned through it in a matter of months without appearing to have benefited from the cash infusion. "What happened to it?"

"I had some debts. Back rent. And…and a friend needed help. Mr. Quinn, I come from the Downtown Eastside. I've lived here my whole life. Where else was I supposed to go?"

It was clear she'd gone to Marnie, who stepped closer to her side. She laid a possessive hand on Kellie's shoulder. She offered Caleb a sneer. "I got her a SRO at the Balmoral. Kept her safe."

Lovely.

It nauseated him to think of her in one of those rooms. "It's going to be pretty hard to raise a baby in a single room occupancy suite with a communal bathroom down the hall. Which leads to the question: What now?"

Silence. It swelled until everyone in the room was inhaling the heavy weight of it. Sophie averted her gaze, Kellie blinked back tears. Marnie patted Kellie's shoulder.

Marnie broke the silence. "We can make it work. We'll find a way."

Kellie lifted her eyes to meet Caleb's. "If I want child support?"

The cynic in him was relieved they were finally getting to the reason he'd been included in this whole sordid mess. "Whether you want it or not, it's his responsibility to provide it. But first we'll need to do DNA testing to prove paternity."

"And then?" There was no hesitation, no question as to the result. She believed, or knew, the baby was Jason's.

"If he's the father he's required by law to pay child support until he's eighteen or is legally adopted by a step-parent. Even if he voluntarily relinquishes his parental rights and wants no access or contact."

Kellie sagged back against the bed.

"He has to support him." Marnie smiled and Caleb knew the hint of triumph and calculation weren't paranoia on his part.

He gritted his teeth so hard his jaw ached. "First things first, we need to prove he's the father."

If what she said was true, another side of the man he knew lived behind the perfect smile, the perfect life. It was brutal, vindictive, and dark.

"Do I need to talk to him, to see him?" asked

Kellie.

"We'll worry about it later. First, you need some rest." Sophie reached over and pulled up the slipping sheet. She ran a hand over Kellie's hair. "You're wrong, you know. You are brave. Don't ever forget it. Now you should get some rest. We'll figure this out. We'll find a way to keep you both safe. Jason Drummond isn't above the law."

She turned to Caleb and dipped her head in the direction of the door. Once they were outside with the door closed she rubbed her arms and met his gaze. "This can't be easy for you. Thank you for listening. For staying. I know you had better things to do."

"Wow." Her low opinion of him hit him square in the gut. He scrubbed a hand over his jaw and blinked away the mental and physical exhaustion. His irritation rose at her assumptions, her desire to see him as nothing more than a sum of his possessions, for pegging him as privileged and callous. "Better things to do? Than coming to the aid of a desperate young girl? I'm flattered."

"I didn't mean it as a put down."

"Yeah, you did. You're not the only one who helps people through tough times." All of a sudden he'd had enough. Tired down to his bones, he didn't care if he was overreacting. "I practice family law for a reason. I provide support through a very difficult period in people's lives. We analyze choices, try to resolve difficult conflicts, and I ensure they have a legally binding agreement when it's said and done. All with the least amount of pain possible. Because I know what it's like to watch your family fall apart. To be the pawn in a game of custody chess. I do my best to make sure those situations don't happen in my office, with my clients, no matter their billing address."

"I'm sure you do good work."

They were back to first meeting status: stilted, wary, and uncomfortable. The hell with that. "Damn right I do. And I don't require your recognition or praise to sleep at night. But thank you for acknowledging I'm not quite the selfish, privileged bastard you assumed I was."

"I never said you were a bastard."

"But you thought it."

She crossed her arms. "Now who's making assumptions?"

He pushed a hand through his hair. This was getting them nowhere. He pointed at the closed door. "The man they're talking about in there? He would never…"

Sophie's lips thinned. "You don't believe her?"

Calm, rational, and quick thinking were all traits he valued and cultivated. Right now he felt none of those things.

"I need time to figure some things out." He shoved his hands inside his pockets. "Because do you? Unquestionably, without-a-doubt believe everything they've said? You're too smart to take what they're saying on faith."

Her brows rose. "I'm smart enough to know you've got a conflict of interest. You need to decide whether you can proceed fairly and objectively. Because yes, I believe her. Why would she lie to us?"

God help him, her chin went up. Her eyes flashed with her need to take him down a peg. His fingers clenched inside his pockets. Her challenge, the heat of it, inspired absolute honesty.

"Because anyone who knows you or who's familiar with your work knows you'll do whatever it takes, go balls to the wall, to champion a victimized young woman from the Low Track. And if taking sides hands you a chance to take down the man who's determined to clean up the Downtown Eastside, all the better. Jason Drummond is pain in your ass. Of course, they came to you." And hell, since he was destroying any chance at a relationship he might as well go for it. "And I don't know what your history is with Marnie, but you're doing it as much for her as you are for Kellie. So maybe I need to be the one asking, how objective are you?"

"You see me as a do-gooder who doesn't question facts, just reacts. Part of my job requires cutting through all the bullshit and believe me, I hear a lot of it. I'm a great lie-detector. Don't confuse nonjudgmental with sucker. And, yes, Marnie is important to me. But I can be her friend and know she's not perfect, far from it. I know even if I believe Kellie about paternity, I'll need to double check anything coming out of Marnie's mouth." She inhaled a deep breath. Let it out. "Because…Marnie…she doesn't have the greatest track record with the truth."

The dejection in her tone tugged at him. He resisted moving in closer. She had scoffed away all his attempts to explain Tiffany. She didn't want to believe him. Or in him. "Just because Jason is a friend of mine doesn't mean I'm not interested in getting to the truth." He pointed at the door. "Or doing what's best for that child in there. So let's agree we both have agendas, but we're most interested in the truth."

****

Fine, bring on the truth. What to do with it was the problem. Sophie tried to rub some warmth back into her arms. What to do about Caleb Quinn? She wanted to trust him. It was in the tightening of her stomach. In the flush of her skin when he touched her. Which he seemed to do every chance he got. He was a toucher. And she craved touch. Her libido, in hibernation since Liam, woke. And it was all Caleb's fault.

"The truth," she agreed.

One problem at a time. Did Jason Drummond pay to have sex with young girls? Was the proof in the tiny room behind her? When she thought of the rhetoric he spewed, the harm he was doing to the Downtown Eastside with his gentrification plans, she wanted to hurl. His calls for tough solutions and increased policing? Who was going to police him?

Stop him?

She was bound by confidentiality. By ethics. Damn it. She opened her mouth.

Caleb held up a hand. "It's enough for tonight."

Fine. But there was one more thing she needed to know. "Why did you come here tonight?"

Because despite the trauma of the evening and their being on opposite sides, she was glad he was here. He was a rational, organized thinker. One who listened and guided, allowing Kellie to articulate her story. To feel safe in the telling. It was one of the sexiest qualities in the history of men. Oh yes, she so wanted to trust him.

He frowned, like he didn't quite approve of the change in topic. Like the answer was a given so why was she even asking. "I thought you were in trouble."

"And that's all there was to it? Why didn't you call the police?" Was the answer so simple? To help her out. To make sure she was safe when usually she was the one doing the saving.

His jaw muscle jumped. "What kind of white knight would that make me?"

"I didn't imagine you'd come." More truth. In fact, she'd never expected to hear from him again. Not after she'd shut him down so completely.

"Then you don't know me as well as you think you do." The incremental shake of his head, the slight tightening of his mouth added to his look of wounded warrior. The implication being, of course, this wasn't the first time she'd jumped to the wrong conclusion.

"You're right. I don't." She'd misjudged him. His ability to ease a tense situation, his way of dealing with Marnie, was nothing short of amazing. She'd counted on discounting him, instead she was impressed. The one man she'd committed to hadn't understood medicine was more than her career but her passion. Caleb understood the distinction. She'd felt it when he'd talked about his job. Yes, it was more than a shame Caleb wasn't her type. "But in my defense, you don't wear armor or carry a sword."

"Don't let the suit fool you. It's Teflon-coated." He tilted his head and the heat in his direct look warmed her belly. "I want a chance to get to know you. To show you who I am."

Casual relationships weren't her thing. Once she'd yearned for more. For the commitment other women scoffed at. Then she'd learned her lesson. It didn't mean she didn't crave family. She refused to ask about the woman from his office. It was none of her business. Neither was he. But renewed determination to resist him didn't mean he wasn't getting to her.

No soft music played. The dim lighting was courtesy of an unlit dingy hallway. The smell of antiseptic and desperation laced the air. It didn't matter. Sophie wanted to meet his challenge. She didn't want to dodge. Or object. She wanted to kiss the hell out of Caleb Quinn.

So she stepped back. "I can't do this with you. I need to know I matter. That I'm the only name on your list."

Caleb took her face in his warm hands. "Sophie, right now there is no one else but you."

She wrapped her hands around his wrists and tugged them away. "But there's a long line behind me and I'm choosing not to join the queue."

"Don't." He refused to let go of her hands when she tried to release them, brought them up between them. "Don't toss this aside."

"I don't do casual."

"There won't be anything casual about it."

She believed him. But his kind of temptation could cause havoc. Distraction. Devastation. He was already a virus in her blood. "There's something else you should know about me. I don't compromise on my ideals. I need someone who shares my beliefs. Supports them."

Caleb ran a thumb over her bottom lip. "Why do I feel like I've been insulted?"

Her lips lifted at the corners. "We don't fit, Caleb. You have to know it."

His hand slid around her waist as he stepped closer, brought her against him. "We fit fine."

She brushed a hand across his brow, straightened his hair, before resting it over his heart. "Not where it counts."

He put a hand over hers, held it in place when she would have pulled free. "Don't confuse guarded with conniving bastard."

Touché.

"I need to go back in there." For no good reason she thought of the new outfit hanging in her closest. She'd bought it with the express intention of kicking his ass tonight. Instead he'd turned the tables on her, stirring up urges she'd never expected to feel. Not for him.

"Word of warning. I'm not giving up. You fascinate me, Doctor Monroe." He smoothed a finger across her cheek, along her jaw, her throat. "I want to get to know you. I want to debate philosophy with you, naked in bed, then again over breakfast. I want to take you to dinner. Watch a movie with you. Naked in bed."

She braced her hands against his chest. "I get it. You're a closet nudist."

He laughed. "See what I mean. Who could resist you?"

She snorted. "Plenty of people, as it turns out."

"I meant what I said."

"So did I. But back to reality, I need to check on Kellie and the baby. Get them ready for transport. It can't be much longer."

He spread his hands. "I'll help any way I can."

"Thank you for that generous offer." She smiled. This was going to be fun. A little revenge for turning over her engine with no hope of leaving the garage. "You can give Marnie a ride to the hospital. She won't be able to ride in the ambulance."

He stiffened, shook his head, his smile slipping away. "No. No way."

"She'll want to go. I've never seen her attach herself to someone like she has with Kellie. And Kellie needs her." She thought of the samples she needed to send away for testing. The absence of needle marks on Kellie reassured her, but she held onto her worry. There were ways and if Marnie was involved…

She turned toward the loud knocking coming from the backdoor entry and was relieved to see the flashing lights of the ambulance. "Here we go."

****

Caleb reached for a can of soup from Sophie's impressive collection. Kellie and baby were in the hospital, at least overnight. Marnie had wanted to stay with them, except it had taken her less than sixty seconds to piss off every nurse or attendant in the vicinity. More than once during the admission process he'd thought of the illegal weapon he had stashed in his glove compartment and how he'd like to ask her very nicely, at gun point, to shut the fuck up.

He pulled open a drawer, shut it. Opened another. Success. Can opener in hand he did the same with cupboard doors until he located a pot. He had insisted on driving them back to Sophie's. It had made sense, his being the only vehicle capable of making the snow slicked journey. Marnie and Sophie had disappeared down the hall. Caleb was doing his best to ignore Marnie's raised voice, Sophie's hushed one. He scanned the directions on the can before dumping the contents into the pot and waited until it bubbled. Even Doc Sophie, as he'd heard her called at the hospital, had to eat. Someone needed to ensure it happened.

By the look of things she didn't spend any more time in her kitchen then he did in his. An empty cereal bowl kept company with her half-finished mug of coffee. Her black and white skull and crossbones cookie jar sat empty. A cookbook lay open on the counter and her fridge held the contents of things necessary for a small Christmas dinner.

Hard to believe it was Christmas Day. He was expected to spend half the day with his mother, the other half with his father. No peace or goodwill existed on those two fronts, at least when it came to each other.

The scent of tinned soup and over processed tomatoes followed him around the rest of her tiny ground-level garden suite. Specks of color flashed from different places. Pillows, candles, and the bits and pieces of female flotsam left lying around. But the showstopper was the introspective framed black-and-white photographs arranged in clusters on the deep blue walls. A photo journal of the Downtown Eastside, they told a tale of boarded up buildings, the flash of new businesses, the Empress Hotel on Hastings, St. Paul's on Cordova, her clinic's back alley mural, and people. In every season. One in particular caught his eye.

Sophie rounded the corner and paused by his side. She offered a tired smile. "I only know him by his street name, Chain Man. He carries those every day, all day, as penance."

The ropes of industrial chain looped around his neck bowed his shoulders. It was a lot of baggage to haul around. "For what?"

She shrugged. "No one knows. Or they're not sharing the reason with me."

He ran a finger down the side of a frame showing an elderly woman pushing a black cat in an ancient baby stroller. "Each one tells a story."

Silence settled around them. She shot him a glance then faced the wall once again. "Thank you."

"I made some soup." He noted her tired eyes and knew he should leave, let her get some sleep. But he held back, reluctant to let her out of his sight. "Some for Marnie too. If she's hungry."

"I don't care if she is or not." She rolled her eyes. "I'm not going back in there to ask. I think we've had enough quality time together for one day. I'm going to make some tea. Do you want some?" She headed to the tiny galley kitchen, filled the kettle with water and put it on the stove.

Tea? He never drank tea. He mainlined caffeine the traditional way, from a to-go cup. No woman had ever offered to make him tea. Not his mother, who survived on organic juices suffused with an indecent amount of kale. Certainly not his grandmother who swilled coffee in the morning and gin the rest of the day. She was eighty-one so who was he to judge. But if drinking tea meant staying a few extra minutes, he'd drink tea. "Sure, why not."

With the tea steeping they settled in at the kitchen table over bowls of soup and a plate of honest-to-God homemade chocolate chip cookies she pulled from the freezer section of her fridge. Courtesy of a patient she explained. It was warm, cozy, and a little bit terrifying. Certainly not the seduction he'd planned.

He dipped his head in the direction of her wall art. "You're very talented."

"Thank you." Cup in hand she settled back into her chair. "It's a hobby of mine."

"They're amazing." *You're amazing*. He shifted in his chair. Nope, not going there. Not tonight.

She offered up a tired half-smile. "It's easy being on my side of the camera."

"So why the Downtown Eastside?"

She shrugged. "Why not?"

"Those photographs suggest there's more to it than casual happenstance."

"So, in other words what's a nice girl like me doing on the wrong side of the tracks?" She set her mug down on the table with a soft thud.

He changed tactics. Conversation, like chess, involved knowing when to capture, exchange, or evade. "If you'd rather not tell me that's okay. Obviously, you have very personal reasons."

"You're very clever, aren't you?" Sophie grimaced. She picked up a cookie and nibbled. Caleb sipped his lukewarm tea and waited.

"Anyways, it doesn't matter." She sighed. Her voice lowered and Caleb leaned in to hear. "My sister disappeared from our home town when I was ten and she was eighteen. It wasn't until years later we found out she was living in Vancouver. My parents never tried to make contact—my sister was…difficult. They insisted she knew where they lived if she wanted to see them. God knows, it was easier without her there. When I came here to study medicine, I searched for her in what limited free time I could scrounge."

He thought of the scarred woman behind the closed door just down the hall. "Marnie."

She nodded. "I'd given up hope. No one would talk to me, including the police. Women were disappearing out of the Downtown Eastside. There were rumors of a serial killer. But back then no one with the clout to do anything about it saw Robert Pickton as anything but a pig farmer."

"Sophie." He was sorry he asked. This was too personal, too heartbreaking, and he was a stranger. His ulterior motives bubbled up like acid reflux. He wanted to concede the game that was anything but anymore. "I'm sorry."

She set her half-eaten cookie down on her plate, brushed off her fingertips. "Then one day I found her. She was a mess, drug addicted, homeless. Her mental illness issues untreated." She smiled even as she sniffed back tears she immediately brushed away. "She made it very clear she didn't want anything to do with me."

He offered a smile he didn't feel. "Let me guess, you persisted."

She nodded, straightened her shoulders. "And in doing so found my place. I'm needed here. What I do matters."

"The scars on her face?"

Sophie's gaze landed somewhere past his right shoulder. She lifted an absent hand to her face and traced a line from her ear to the corner of her mouth. Her swallow tracked a path down her lovely neck. "That's not my story to tell."

"Fair enough." Did he even want to know?

"What about you? What matters to you?" Her gaze settled on him and didn't waiver.

She was countering with a move of her own, looking ahead to putting him into check because she didn't think much did. He wondered what she'd do if he mentioned her. Suggested she mattered more than was comfortable. More than was reasonable. How fast would he find himself out in the snow?

"Justice. Fairness. Liberty." Chess was his game

and he still had a few moves left. "We're not so different, you and I."

She laughed, clearly not convinced. "When did you realize you wanted to be a lawyer?"

"I was fourteen, entering grade eight, when my parents sent me away to boarding school."

"The prestigious kind or the ball-busting kind."

"Shawnigan."

Her brows shot up. "Prep school. Nice."

"Yes, well, sending me away to school was the most loving thing they could have done. They gave me the family they couldn't be. There I finally found the structure I needed. It was about tradition, hard work, and expectation. It taught me the need for rules, the need to be a just and fair person."

"So out of expected doctor, lawyer, entrepreneur you picked lawyer?"

"The noblest of noble professions."

"And just when we were starting to get along." She wrinkled her nose. Wrapped her hands around her mug of tea. "Let me guess, you met Jason Drummond there."

She was closing in on his queen and he wasn't quite sure how it had happened. "He was a couple of years ahead of me, but we hit it off. We were on the rowing team together."

"And you're friends. You trust him?"

Checkmate.

"Trust is a strong word." He'd played a sloppy game. Then again his intention hadn't been to win, but to observe how she played the game. Could he trust her? The answer surprised him so he answered. "His wife is a good friend. We get together for drinks, see each other at different functions. He's continued on his family's tradition as reputable builders…"

"But?"

He shook his head. "He's driven. Competitive. He's got his hand in so many pies I don't know how he keeps track. Or when he sleeps."

"Is it possible Marnie and Kellie are telling the truth? Not about paternity, but about the rest of it?" She didn't quite meet his eye.

"Does Jason Drummond arrange to have sex with young girls barely legal enough to qualify as adults? Threaten them?" He didn't want to believe it. Caleb had learned long ago wishing a person lived up to your expectations didn't make it so. He kept further opinions about Jason to himself. "I think there's more to the story. Something they're not telling us."

"Such as?"

"It's our job to find out. All part of piecing the puzzle together." She tried to hide a yawn and he was reminded of the hour. He got up and offered her his hand. "Time for bed."

She fluttered her eye lashes with faked vigor. "But we've only had one date."

He tugged on her hand until she was standing flush against him. "This counts." He gestured to the table. "Food, drinks, and I want points for sharing."

"Goodnight, Caleb." Her sleepy smile tugged at his heart.

He lowered his head. "Sweet dreams, Sophie."

She didn't want to deal with his kiss. It was in her tired eyes. He gathered her in closer, ran a hand over her hair, and closed the gap. She sagged in complete fatigue. Her lips parted in protest, but he bypassed them to drop a kiss on her cheek. He pulled back a little and she followed his lead. She smoothed her hands over his shirt without making eye contact. He ran a hand over her hair before grabbing his jacket and heading for the door.

He paused just outside her open doorway. "Goodnight, Sophie."

"Goodnight, Caleb." Then she shut the door in his face.

He pulled up the collar of his coat and whistled a Christmas tune all the way to his vehicle. Life was about to get messy, which was fine by him. The night had given him a mission and Sophie as a partner. He glanced up at the now clear sky with it diffusion of stars and gave thanks for the best Christmas gift ever.

Chapter Three

Sophie assumed it was Caleb's doing. This morning her car was parked on the street outside her apartment, towed from her clinic's parking lot sometime in the night. Unless he moonlighted as a tow truck driver she had no idea how he'd pulled it off. She didn't have access to his kind of pull. Or money. It left her even more in his debt. Which was unacceptable. How did you pay back a man who has everything and respect yourself in the morning?

How was she supposed to stop thinking about him when he pulled this kind of crap?

Not that she wasn't grateful. She'd picked up Kellie and baby from the hospital late in the afternoon. She wanted Kellie here where she could keep an eye on her. Marnie too. She'd spent the morning borrowing a car seat, playpen, diapers, and some baby clothes. Thank God for friends. And she couldn't have done it without her vehicle.

Once they were home, it was pointers on taking care of baby. Conversations about babies. Getting baby to sleep. To eat. Another long and exhausting day that also included cooking a meal fit for baby's first Christmas Day. No pressure there. Three adults in residence and not one of them knew how to produce a meal that hadn't come from a can, come prepackaged and frozen, or ordered by phone. The real miracle would be escaping food poisoning. Sophie longed for bed and some quiet time. Fed up didn't even begin to describe it. Thanks to Marnie.

"I want Drummond to leave her alone," demanded Marnie. She paced Sophie's tiny kitchen, her frustration building. Sophie put a silencing finger to her lips. Kellie and baby were in the spare room down the short hall. Both sleeping last time she checked.

"Don't shush me."

Sophie shoved the plastic-wrapped plate of leftover dry roast chicken in the fridge. Outside her kitchen window a smattering of stars lit up the night sky as frost crept in from the four corners of the old style window. She petitioned the biggest and brightest for patience.

"Everything's going to be fine." Sophie was not in the mood for another rant. She shoved the salt and pepper shakers at her sister. "They go over there."

Marnie yanked open a cupboard door. "You have no idea what he's capable of."

Didn't she? She'd been served the list over breakfast, lunch, and dinner. Sophie grabbed a stack of plates and opened the dishwasher. The clatter of filling it drowned out the whine of her sister's voice for five blessed minutes.

"There, almost done." She tossed a dishcloth at Marnie. "Wipe down the table. I'll make tea."

Tea made everything better in Sophie's opinion.

"I don't want a cup of tea." Marnie ignored the wet cloth in favor of picking at a thread escaping from the frayed hem of her hoodie. The one she refused to take off.

"No more caffeine." She eyed the extra gigantic to-go cup by Marnie's side. She'd slipped out while

Sophie helped Kellie put Quinn to sleep. She didn't want to think about what else she'd gone out for.

"Would you stop! You're not my damn mother."

"I'm just trying to help." It was all she'd ever wanted, to help make life easier for her sister.

"No. You don't. You want to take over my life. Change it until I don't recognize it anymore."

"I want you to be healthy. To take your meds. To realize I'm trying to help you."

"Yeah? Fuck my meds. They don't work anyway. They make me feel…funny, clumsy. I'm not letting your precious pills mess with my head."

No, instead she'd mess with Sophie's. "Then we can make an appointment to get them adjust—"

"No. I can look after myself. I'm the big sister, remember? Me." She stabbed a finger into her scrawny chest.

"I remember." But who could blame her if she forgot the fact Marnie was eight years her senior. "Nobody's saying you can't look after yourself."

"Damn right you are. It's a freaking constant buzz in my head." Marnie flung out her hands and waved them around like the buzz was outside her head too. "Do this. See this doctor. Go here. It should be me helping you. I'm the oldest. It's supposed to be my job to look after us."

"Fine." Sophie held up a conciliatory hand. "We'll talk. Have a conversation. Tell me how you broke your wrist?"

"It's nothing. I fell." Marnie tugged at her sleeve, pulled it down over the tips of her fingers. Her eyes mapped a frantic search of the kitchen. A flip switched. She changed topic. "I don't know how much longer we can stay here. He could find us. When he does there'll be trouble."

"How's he going to find you? Jason Drummond has no idea where Kellie is, or that she's even given birth." Sophie slipped past her to fill the kettle with water. "Besides it's Christmas Day. I'm sure he's occupied spending time with family."

"In his gated McMansion, with his eight hundred foot Christmas tree and mountain of presents." She jabbed a finger in the direction of the back of the apartment. "What about his son? Shouldn't he be concerned about him?"

Sophia reached into the cupboard for some tea bags. The whole story was too bizarre. Jason Drummond's family was the closest thing the west coast had to royalty. They occupied the biggest houses in the choicest neighborhoods. He was movie star handsome. The black sheep, badass, or bad boy label had never applied. And she was supposed to believe he'd paid money to have sex with Kellie? Tossed her to the street for fathering his child?

"He's a psychopath."

"Marnie." Sophie closed the cupboard door with a snap. She'd seesawed between the opposite demands all day but it had cranked up since she'd come back with Kellie. "We'll make sure Kellie and Quinn are looked after."

"He should have to pay." Marnie accompanied each word with a rap of her finger on the countertop. "To provide for him."

Too tired to care if she was making things worse, Sophie snapped. "Which one is it? Do you want him in her life or out of her life? You can't have it both ways."

The doorbell rang startling them both. Marnie snatched up the chef's knife from the draining board on the counter. The transformation from whiny to aggressive shocked her. Fear leeched out of her sister and into Sophie.

"Put the knife down." Aiming for calm, she tried to keep her voice level. Sophie motioned to the countertop, her heart pounding. "Right now."

"No way." Marnie slipped the knife behind her back and shook her head. "Not until I know who it is."

The doorbell chimed again.

"Now," Sophie insisted. Marnie didn't move, didn't relinquish the knife. "You're scaring me. Is this was you want? For people to be afraid of you?"

Marnie said nothing. Did nothing, but focus her attention in direction of the front door.

Sophie inched toward the small side panel window. She caught sight of Caleb and sighed with relief. "It's Caleb, no one to worry about. Put the knife down."

She waited hand shaking over the knob until she complied. When she stepped back to open the door her heart was jackhammering against her breastbone.

"Hey." He came through the door on a blast of cold air, arms full of bags. So solid, and heaven help her, sane. She hesitated a second, absorbing the notion of him. She needed capable and cool headed right now. He smiled, then a frown slipped in to replace it. "Is everything okay?"

"Yes. It's all good." Sophie swiped her hands over her yoga pants, before pushing up the sleeves of the bulky sweater she'd worn against the chill. "What are you doing here?"

"You're sure you're okay?" He handed her the

packages, craned his neck to see around her into the quiet apartment. "I'm dropping off some stuff I was able to gather together. Thought you could use the extra supplies."

"Just your typical Monroe Christmas around here." She juggled the packages, stepping back to let him in the living room. When was the last time she'd checked in with a mirror? "Thank you."

"Don't thank me yet. The only places open are gas stations." The heat in his smile calmed the anxiety in hers.

He had the whole gorgeous thing going on, casual and urban in dark jeans and a leather jacket. He shrugged out of his coat. He jammed it over one of the overflowing hooks and took back some of his packages. He smelled even better. A combination of power suits and the tropics, like sandalwood and citrus. She wanted to stay in the chilly tiny entryway and breathe him in.

She didn't know what to think of the possessive hand he placed low on her back. Neither did Marnie. At the sight of them walking into the kitchen she crossed her arms and glowered.

Marnie jabbed a finger in Caleb's direction, her eyes accusing Sophie. "What's he doing here?"

"Marnie." Sophie gritted her teeth and sent a warning glare in her direction. She also picked up the knife and stashed it in a drawer, making a mental note to lock them all away.

Marnie ignored her and scowled at Caleb. "Slumming?"

"Merry Christmas to you too." He reached into a plastic bag and pulled out a carton of cigarettes, held them out. "Your brand I believe."

Marnie's eyes narrowed. She hesitated a moment before reaching out for them. Caleb set them in her hand but didn't let go. "You care about Kellie. You want to protect her. I get it. It's even admirable." He cocked his head to continue their eye contact. "But I'm not the enemy. I'm not guilty by association any more than you are."

"Meaning?" Marnie gave a little tug but he still didn't let go of the cigarettes.

"I won't make assumptions about you and your lifestyle if you agree to do the same for me."

Never one to give an inch Marnie surprised her and offered up a slight nod. Caleb let go. He reached into another bag and pulled out a bottle of wine. This time his smile spelled his intentions out in a soft lift of his lips. As in later, over a glass, we'll get to know each other much, much better. "For you."

"Thank you." She put the very expensive bottle of Bordeaux he obviously hadn't purchased at a fuel stop to the side, wished she could pour a glass and disappear into her bedroom. Close the door, climb into bed with Caleb, and unwrap him from head to toe. Not her usual response to stress and it freaked her out. "Did your family let you off early?"

Caleb checked his watch. "I hope it's not too late to stop by. I wanted to see how everyone was doing. How's Kellie?"

"Hopefully sleeping." There was probably more accusation in those two words then was wise because Caleb raised his eyebrows. Sophie rubbed her aching forehead. "She's doing great. Everything is great."

"Well, this has been nice but I'm out of here." Marnie stuffed her carton of cigarettes back into a bag.

"Wait, where are you going?" Sophie moved to intercept her.

"Like I said, out." Marnie headed for the door and grabbed up the old jacket Sophie had dug up for her. Stuffed her feet into likewise donated boots.

"I don't think leaving is a good idea." The last thing she wanted was her agitated, mentally ill sister wandering around in below-freezing temperatures alone.

"It is if I say it is." Marnie grabbed for the doorknob and opened the door.

Sophie pushed past Caleb. "Hold on a—"

"No, you hold on." Marnie pulled out a wool cap and jammed it on her head.

"Ladies," Caleb interrupted.

Marnie flipped up her middle finger. "Stay out of this."

Sophie was one second away from having had enough. "Lower your voice. You're going to wake everyone up."

"Like I said, outta here." The door banged half shut behind her. It flapped open again on a gust of wind when the latch didn't catch.

"Is everything okay?" Kellie crept into the kitchen, eyes wide and scared.

"Nothing to worry about. Marnie's having a moment." Sophie crossed over and gave her a quick hug while Caleb went to deal with the door.

"Oh. All right." She gave Caleb a nervous look before gesturing behind her. "I should get back."

Caleb pulled a beautifully wrapped present from another bag. "Why don't you join us for a minute?" He held it out to her. "For you. It's not much but I hope you like it."

Kellie hesitated, the promise of a present too tempting to resist. After a glance back, she shuffled across the floor. She slipped into the chair held out by Caleb and kept her head down. "Thank you."

After a wistful glance at the bottle of wine, Sophie took her cue from Caleb. "I'll get some cups. We'll have tea."

Caleb set the present down in front of Kellie. She fingered the bow, the pretty wrapping. He nudged it closer. "Go ahead, open it."

Kellie picked at the tape until the paper floated away from the boutique box. She lifted the lid off and pulled out a bright green baby's quilt. She gathered it up in her hands and held it to her face, closed her eyes. "It's so soft. And beautiful. He'll love it."

Sophie had no idea how he'd managed it and Kellie didn't think to question him. In fact, her grin suggested he'd moved up even further in her ranking of best guy ever.

Sophie studied Caleb, trying her hardest to ignore the ridiculous flutter in her stomach, fearful it was going to get worse. "Wait until you hear the news. We have a name."

Kellie blushed. "Quinn Monroe Andrews."

He picked up Kellie's hand and lifted her knuckles to his lips. "I'm honored to share a name with him."

Sophie was right. Squishy, cheesy Disney moment. Her insides did another little flip. Just how skilled was he at the whole Prince Charming act? And it had to be an act. How often did he use it? She pulled mugs down from the cupboard. Caleb continued to beguile Kellie. Her head came up and she straightened in her chair. She told a cute little Quinn story from earlier in the day. A different person emerged without Marnie around. They all relaxed.

Sophie let the guilt slide away. Marnie would come back. For no other reason than Kellie was here. For some reason she was deeply attached to her. Sophie wanted to know why. The answers might contain the elusive key to her sister she'd searched for her whole life.

****

Caleb slid the plate of cookies closer to Kellie then picked one for himself. It was the perfect time to ask a few questions. They'd see what Kellie had to say without her shadow around. "You and Marnie are pretty close?"

"Close as sisters." She smiled than realized what she'd said. She shot guilty look in Sophie's direction. "Kind of like it anyway."

"How long have you known each other?"

"Her and my dad used to hook up sometimes." She picked at her fingernails. "Long time ago."

"Is he in the picture now? Your father?"

"No." She shook her head. "I don't where he is. He's like that, you know? Here one minute, then something comes up."

"It must be hard?" Caleb couldn't imagine a life free of parental intrusion. His parents had quarreled over every detail of his young life. Loud, bitter arguments over where he went, who he went with, how he got there.

"I guess." Kellie shrugged. Her head went down. She rubbed the palms of her hands over her sweatpants. "Anyways, I should get back to Quinn." She held up the blanket. "Thanks."

"You're welcome." Caleb smiled to ease the tension. She didn't return it. "Why don't you sit for a little longer? So we can talk. The sooner we get things settled for Quinn the better."

"I think I should wait for Marnie."

Caleb leaned forward. He kept his voice low, soft. "You can talk things over with her when she gets back. It's not going to hurt to talk to Sophie and I. We're here to help."

Kellie hesitated. "I should really wait for Marnie."

Sophie reached over and refilled her mug with tea. She pulled up a chair, ran a hand over Kellie's back. "Marnie will be back. But the sooner we know what you want, the sooner we can work on making it happen."

Caleb rested his forearms on the table and clasped his hands around his cup. "This is my job. This is what I do. I help people through these kinds of situations. And I can help you, but you have to tell me what you want."

Still she wavered.

"As your lawyer I'm bound by solicitor-client privilege. What you disclose is protected information. This way I can do the best possible job for you. You can trust me."

Tears filled her eyes and she whispered, "I want to keep my baby."

"It comes to this. You had no legal relationship with the father. Unless there is a court order to the contrary, the mother is presumed to have sole guardianship of the child, and the parent presumed to have custody of the child is the parent with whom the child usually lives. That's you."

"What…what happens if I want him to pay me money? You know? Like child support?"

"Then contact will be made with Jason Drummond. He'll involve his lawyers. The first thing his lawyer will do is request a paternity test. So I'm going to ask you one more time and then I'll drop it. Is there any possibility at all Jason Drummond is not Quinn's father?"

The tip of her ponytail swung back and forth. Her cheeks flushed a pretty shade of pink. Caleb's gut squeezed and his hand tightened around his mug. The idea of a grown man, someone he called friend, taking advantage of her repulsed him on every level.

Caleb tried to relax, wanted to keep his body language loose, open. He pulled in a deep mental breath. "If he's the biological father, he has a legal responsibility to pay support."

"Do I have to see him?"

"I'm not going to let anything happen to you. I promise."

"And afterwards?" Her voice was small and scared. It broke his heart.

"Why don't we take this one step at a time?" Jason Drummond wasn't going to want to have anything to do with Quinn Andrews or his mother. Still Caleb had to ask. "Do you want Quinn to have a relationship with his father?"

She pushed up her sleeves and for the first time that night met his look head on. "He tossed me aside like I was garbage. He doesn't care about me or Quinn. He's worried about what the rest of the world will think if they find out about us. He's going to do whatever it takes to make sure that doesn't happen."

Caleb wanted to disagree, but he never lied to his clients. "I'm not going to let him hurt you."

"You fight fair. He doesn't." She picked up the blanket, gave it a squeeze. Her smile was sweet and in her ponytail and sweats she looked innocent and fragile. Her true age was in her eyes, suggesting he was the naïve one. "He saw me as a plaything. As disposable. That's what he paid for. I wish I didn't have to see him again. Or take his money. That I could fix things on my own. But I can't."

"Kellie,—"

"I'll take your help because I have to and because I want to do what's best for my family." She pushed back from the table. "Thanks for the present."

Sophie frowned after a retreating Kellie. "What do you make of that?"

Caleb scrubbed a hand over the back of his neck and tried to ease the tension pooling between his shoulders. "I want to know who she means by family."

"How do you think Jason Drummond's going to react to having to pay child support?"

"I meant what I said." He put a hand on her arm and heated up a little on the inside when she swung those beautiful green eyes his way. "He's done hurting her. Or anyone else."

"That's one loaded guarantee." The intensity of her search for his true meaning was a jab to his midsection.

She didn't trust him. The notion derailed him for a second, but only a second. "It's a promise."

"And just how do you plan to deliver on it?"

"By using the law."

She tilted her head, studied him, let out a little puff

of breath. "Okay. How can I help?"

"Try and get Kellie to open up, see if she'll give up some more details. Like who makes the arrangements. There's got to be a pimp in the background somewhere. Find out what Marnie knows."

Her gaze wavered for a moment. She looked away, pulled in her bottom lip, bit down. Then she was back focusing in on him again. Her jaw tightened and her eyes flashed. "You were here earlier. She doesn't talk to me. She puts up with me from time to time when she needs something."

"Not to sound insensitive but she definitely has a vested interest in this situation. She needs things to work out for Kellie's sake. Ask her why?"

Her smile was bitter. "I'll try."

"It's been a long day and I could use a drink." He got up and opened the glass fronted cabinet. Two wineglasses in hand, he grabbed the bottle of wine. "Corkscrew?"

She sat back, a small smile tipped up the corners of her mouth. "What's the matter, only coal in your stocking this morning?"

"On the contrary, my mother bought me a race horse." The corkscrew was in the first drawer he opened.

A stifled cough. "That was nice of her."

"Yeah, except it's a little large for my condo. And there'll be hell to pay when I return it. Anyways, she didn't give it to me because I was into horseracing. Every year she tries to outdo my father's annual gift of box season tickets to the Canucks."

"Gee, all I got was a bottle of wine."

"And the best part of my day was giving it to you."

The cork slid out of the bottle. He poured a small amount into each glass and handed one to her. "What do you think?"

She sniffed, raised an eyebrow. "Somewhat bold for my tastes."

"Not mine." He swirled the wine around in his glass without taking his eyes off her. Sipped. "Great body. The promise of a strong personality. Intense flavor."

She tipped her glass, examined the contents. "Really? Your taste buds are very intuitive."

He'd waited all day for the chance to see her again. To talk to her. "If a person wasn't careful he'd be very tempted to overindulge."

"And regret it in the morning." Sophie lifted her glass to her lips.

"Never." He set his glass down. Moved in closer. Lifted her glass out of her hand and set it down beside his on the kitchen table. It had proved very sturdy in his fantasies. Fantasies that had heated up the few brief hours of sleep he'd managed to catch after leaving Sophie. He coaxed her to her feet. "The idea is to pace yourself. Draw it out. Take the time to savor. Make it last all night."

Sophie put a hand on his chest. "Caleb."

"Sophie." He set his mouth on hers and waited. When her lips parted, he closed his eyes in gratitude. Soft at first, his tongue danced with hers. The spicy taste of the wine went straight to his head.

Her fingertips dug into his shoulder blades. Her mouth opened wide under his giving him more room to play. She was flush against him, warm and yielding. His hands slid underneath her baggy sweater and found heated flesh. He forgot about house guests and sleeping babies and focused on uncovering more skin. On getting her sweater off along with whatever else was underneath it.

"Caleb."

The urgent whisper of his name brought him back. His hands stilled over her bare back. Her hands moved up to rest on either side of his face. When he opened his eyes, hers were still closed, her breath coming out in little puffs of air. He rested his forehead on hers. "Come home with me."

"I can't." He felt her sigh. "Kellie needs me here. She's still new at this and feeling very insecure. I can't leave, no matter how much I want to. And I'm not sure I'm ready for this. For us."

He was ready enough for both of them. Caleb figured she was also worried about Marnie. Because she was worried she'd wait up for her. However long it took.

His hands still rested against her skin. He ached to explore. She was so close. Another tattoo peeked out from under her sweater. He wanted to trace its path, hear its story.

But tonight wasn't the night. He let her go but took her hand. Her nails short, her fingers long, they curled around his. He brought her knuckles to his lips.

"You're going to dream of me. Nothing sweet. Those dreams are going to make you toss and turn." His other hand brushed her cheek. "There's heat between us and making excuses not to feel it isn't going to satisfy either of us. You can trust me. You know you can. Have the courage to admit it."

He left her standing there openmouthed and

confused. Good. He wanted her to come to him for the answers. And hopefully he left her wanting and aching. Just like him.

****

Sophie settled in and opened the album. The plastic pages crinkled under her fingers. She flipped past pictures, searched until she found the one she wanted. Liam had his arms wrapped around her waist. The sea was behind them. They shared wide smiles for the camera. A shiny new diamond ring flashed on her finger. She sucked at relationships. Big time. Take Liam. She had wanted to have him and to hold him and make babies with him. She'd wanted marriage right up until the day before their wedding when he'd called things off. It would be a mistake he'd said. All her passion was channeled into her career. Marnie would always be a problem. She wasn't emotionally available to him.

The memory of his words soured the sweet lingering taste of Caleb. What did she know about relationships or being a family? Except failure? Sophie returned to the front of the album, stroked a finger over a faded photo. They looked happy, her parents, Marnie and her. They smiled for the camera. A Christmas tree strung with tinsel and her grandmother's treasured ornaments provided the backdrop. If she tried she could hear the laughter of extended family gathering around. It was the last Christmas they'd spent in the same place before everything broke apart.

Nothing of the fight earlier that long ago day showed on their faces. Not the screaming. Not the slammed doors, angry curse words, or bizarre accusations. Not her mother's weeping.

75

What good did it do to relive it all again? She shut the book and laid it aside. She tucked her feet up under her and pulled the blanket tighter. Her Christmas tree with its multi-colored lights lit up the corner. The television was playing some feel good goofy holiday movie. She turned it off and curled up.

She thought of Caleb. And sex. Of courage. Oh, he was good. Throw down a challenge because Sophie can't resist a challenge. Like he knew her. Had figured out what made her tick. Challenges, compliments, witty repartee. And she was ticking. *If* she decided she was ready, she was going to eat him alive.

Planning out her moves proved an excellent anesthetic. She grinned into her warm blanket, confident she was on the right track. Definitely distracting. Why shouldn't she take a page out of Caleb's book? Keep things casual. Fun. The want pulsed down her nerve endings, her fingers knotted in the knitted spread. She could do it and enjoy every moment. When they were done? They were done. No regrets.

She allowed her eyes to drift shut. It would be so easy to do casual with him. What would he look like unbuttoned and undone? Long and lean she decided as she relaxed against a pillow. She pictured him liking slinky, black lingerie. A black lacy bra to match? And heels. Very high heels. All the better to stab him in the ego.

He was a thinking man, one who knew the power of words, one who would excel at the language of sex. He wasn't scared to get his hands dirty. She'd underestimated him there. She visualized him in court. Like her favorite book. The heat of a stifling courtroom.

The rustle of anxious spectators. Caleb Quinn arguing on behalf of the impossible.

Irresistible.

The lovely fantasy evaporated at the sound of a key fitting into her front door lock. She lifted her head, waited. There was no way for Marnie to avoid her. She was sitting on her makeshift bed.

There were no other lights on except for the lit tree so she sat up and switched on a lamp. Marnie took her time putting away her winter gear.

"You're still up." Marnie's tone backed up her sneer.

"I couldn't sleep." Sophie smoothed a hand over her hair. "And I wanted to talk to you."

"Goodie. Why aren't you off shagging the lawyer?" Marnie came and slumped down into the chair across from Sophie. Her head dropped back and she sighed. "It might go a long way to helping you relax."

"Where have you been?" Sophie searched for signs of drug use, trying to determine if she'd gone to meet her dealer. There was no sweating, no shaking. Not like before she'd stormed off.

"Around." Marnie straightened up. She grabbed up the discarded album, turned a couple of pages and snapped it shut. Tossed it aside. "Checking on some things."

"We need to talk about Kellie."

"God, you are such a pain in the ass." She sniffed, and sniffed again. Sophie's heart sank. Marnie draped her arms over the sides of the cushy chair. "I'll worry about Kellie. I'm going to take care of everything."

The thought of Marnie policing Kellie's situation scared Sophie worse than any rant she could have thrown. Caleb was right. She knew it. Some things were a given. It was up to her to ask the hard questions. "How did the two of you meet?"

"On the street. Where else?" It came out on a sigh as she continued to stare at the ceiling.

"Kellie says you had a relationship with her father."

Marnie tensed and then made a concentrated effort to appear casual. She lifted her head and nodded at the couch. "I'm super tired and you're taking up space on my bed, so…"

"Did you?"

"Did I what?"

"Have a relationship with him?"

"Depends on your definition." Marnie's gaze settled on her. Her warning smile hinted at the coming hurt. "I stayed there whenever he could afford it. The place had four walls, the drugs were quality, and he's hung like a horse. So I, you know, made the most of it."

Sophie refused to react, not so much as a twitch. This was Marnie at her best or worst depending how you looked at it. It didn't mean the hurt didn't go bone deep. "We do what we have to, to survive. No one blames you."

Marnie snorted. "You never give up, do you?"

No, she didn't. It made the question she had to ask next so damn hard. Because there were some things you didn't want the answer to. "What you said about Jason Drummond shopping the DTES? Who lines up the girls for him? Who gets the finder's fee?"

Marnie turned her head to stare at the colored lights of the tree. With a shaky hand she pushed back her hair. She didn't speak. She didn't have to.

"Oh, God." Sophie closed her eyes. Her throat dried up, whispers were all she had left. "How could you?"

"They volunteered, okay? I didn't force them into anything. They went in knowing the score, their eyes wide open." She shifted in the chair. Tried to shrug it off. Appear casual. It didn't work. "In the end they had some money to make a better life."

"And Kellie? This is her better life?" Sophie demanded, opting for anger.

"You don't know anything about her life."

"So, tell me," Sophie pressed. "Enlighten me. I need to know why this girl means so damn much to you."

"Why? Jealous?" It was there in Marnie's eyes. The pinpricks of triumph. The knowledge she'd scored a direct hit.

Sophie tried to swallow the hurt but it came right back up. It grew teeth on its way out of her mouth. "You pimped her out to a man with no more scruples than you. You hate Jason Drummond? Take a good hard look in the mirror."

"Don't you dare compare me to him," Marnie spat out.

"What did you do with the money he gave Kellie? What kind of trouble are you in?"

"I'm not in any kind of trouble. I'm squeaky clean. Can't you tell?"

"You want to ruin your life? Fine. If you care for her so damn much why drag Kellie down with you?"

"I didn't drag her. She volunteered."

"She's eighteen years old. She loves you. She trusts you."

"God, when are you going to wake up! She was this close to being evicted. No money for food. Or clothes. No job experience. It was either Jason Drummond's money or flashing her ass on the street to strangers offering to toss her a twenty for a blow job. So you tell me: What option would you choose?"

"There are places who will take in—"

"It's called reality. And it exists for some of us."

"And you took Kellie's and made it infinitely more complicated. On top of all those challenges you listed she now has a child to care for and protect. Because the man you sold her to isn't going to be happy about being her baby daddy."

"I said I was going to fix it. Make it right."

"You can't even make things right for yourself." Sophie stood, her only desire to put distance between her and her sibling. She'd been jealous, so jealous of Kellie and her relationship with her sister. Now all she saw was one more victim. Halfway to the hallway she halted, turned back. "Merry Christmas. You've gotten what you've always wanted. I give up."

She'd spent her whole life trying to make up for her parents' lack of understanding and their refusal to acknowledge Marnie's mental illness. For their abandonment. For the first time in those collection of years, she was walking away first. It didn't lessen the weight. It only made it harder to drag along behind her.

Chapter Four

Caleb strode into the bar of the Empress Hotel, a grand name for the tall, skinny landmark holding court in the most notorious section of the Downtown Eastside. A brief scan showed no signs of Sophie, so he headed for the front of the cramped room and the empty stools lining the bar. It had taken some convincing but she'd agreed to meet him for a drink after work. Okay, he'd called it a strategy session. She'd picked the spot.

"Not there." A slight tug on his arm steered him to the right. Sophie dipped her head in the direction of an empty table.

"Why not? They're empty." And closer to the alcohol he required after the day he'd spent smoothing things over after his no show on Christmas Eve.

She gave him a look. "They're reserved for regulars. No one else is allowed to sit there."

He stopped to stare at her. "Are you serious?"

She rolled her eyes and led him in the direction of an empty table. "You could always try to sit there and find out."

He sized up the room along with the excellent view of her navigating the way in front of him. He'd half expected her to show up in scrubs but instead dark jeans hugged her hips; a parka with the popular Canada Goose logo hid her curves. Her hair was spiked up and hoops hung from her ears, fur-topped boots protected her feet. She looked like she belonged in front of a roaring fire at a ski lodge.

He shrugged. Right now he was prepared to follow her anywhere. "Lead the way."

Parkas hung from backs of chairs, heads sported varying styles of toque hair. Vancouver was a coastal city and while it might not register north of sixty it was still cold. In Canada winter meant dressing the part.

An elderly man waved. Tattoos ran up his neck and spilled out of his shirt sleeves to cover the backs of his hands. Another man with missing teeth and a wide smile called out, "Hey, Doc." She lifted a hand in recognition, offered a smile here and there. Rested a hand on the shoulder of a woman, leaned in to answer her quiet question. He was starting to think he'd never get a drink when they reached the open table. He pulled out a chair for her.

He settled into the opposite chair, shifted on the hard surface to find a comfortable spot and, if he was honest, to take a second to strategize. It was clear she was in her element. And that he was out of his. No surprise to her since she'd counted on it.

Smart lady. Good thing he relished a challenge. He let the slow burn of hers heat and simmer. Let the hint of smug and the triumphant slide of her tongue over her bottom lip slap at the urges he was keeping locked up tight. She was here to prove a point. He was going to let her. So he raised a brow. "Rough looking crowd."

"Maybe on the outside." She kept busy taking off her coat, stuffing mitts in pockets, placing her pocketbook just so. "But they're simply folks like you and me."

He shot her a look.

"Mostly. Minus the designer suit. And ridiculous watch." She gave his customized Breitling a pointed look. "And the drinks are super cheap."

"Last year's Christmas gift." He shrugged out of his car coat, folded it, and draped it over a chair. "I take it you come here often?"

"Would you think less of me if I said yes?"

"If I admitted it makes me uneasy? Are you going to think less of me?"

She leaned in to point through to the very back. "There's a police station out the rear door. Cops, judges, and clerks have been known to stop in for the occasional beverage."

"Stopping in for a pint at noon is one thing." He dipped his head to the left to study a group of men walking through the door. He recognized gang colors when he saw them. "Ending up here at closing time is another animal entirely."

"Careful, your biases are showing." She signaled a passing waitress then settled back in her chair. "Watch and learn."

The regulars filling those prized bar seats made sure the new arrivals knew they weren't welcome. The staff behind the bar refused to serve them. Cursed with the veil of invisibility they left, but not without a lot of hand gestures and cursing.

"Street Bars 101. The movement of the crowd tells you something. A lot of activity, a lot of walking around, means they're dealing drugs. Working the crowd." She gestured around her. "Look around. What do you see? People sitting and drinking. Content to stay that way. That's how you know a bar is safe."

It bothered him she knew those details. "So, you're

saying there's no difference between here and everywhere else?"

"That's what I'm saying."

The waitress approached and he ordered a much needed beer. He sat back content to play her game and eyed the crowd. "All right, convince me."

She raised an eyebrow. "This isn't a lawyer's idea of foreplay is it?"

"That's privileged information." Truth was she didn't have to do a thing. She breathed, he noticed. Not good but he was too enthralled to care. "Dazzle me."

A delicate frown creased her forehead. Her eyes narrowed the tiniest little bit. He waited her out. She shrugged. "Okay. They're talking about the state of the economy at the next table, the lack of jobs, the price of gas. See those two college girls heading for those reserved bar stools? They're looking for a bit of adventure and slumming it in the DTES. Because they're young and pretty the bartender is going to cut them some slack, offer them a stool, engage in a little flirting. Behind me they're predicting the outcome of the Canucks' next game. Money, women, and sports. What is it you talk about with your buddies over drinks?" She sat back, crossed her arms confident she'd won.

"You've got me there." Caleb debated over his next move when a fuss at the front caught his attention. Three men paused just inside the front of the room. What the *fuck*? He frowned, straightened up and watched Jason Drummond search the room, spot them, and signal to his companions.

And he knew. Without a doubt. Jason Drummond was guilty of everything Kellie accused him of.

"That's it?" Sophie swallowed a sip of beer. She set her glass down. "That was easy."

Caleb gave a slight shake of his head. "Heads up, Jason Drummond just walked in and he's coming this way."

"What?" Her eyes widened with disbelief. She looked toward to the door. There was no way for her to overlook them.

"You can't miss him. He's the tall, overconfident one."

Her disbelief evaporated along with her smile. All the lovely warmth in her eyes died as she swung back to face Caleb. "What's he doing here?"

"I have no idea, but I think we're about to find out."

People paused mid-conversation or mid-drink to check out the new arrivals. It wasn't often black tie came to the Empress. Jason Drummond picked his way through the crowd, lip curled, eyes averted, careful not to brush against anyone or anything.

Caleb stood as the group approached. "Jason. I didn't expect to see you here."

"Your office said you were heading here." He held out a hand for Caleb to shake, offered a smile of confused disdain. "Not your usual stomping grounds."

Caleb motioned to Sophie. "Jason, this is Doctor Monroe."

He turned to Sophie. "We finally meet in person. Even though we've different approaches I like to think we have the neighborhood's best interest at heart. I just wish someone had mentioned how beautiful you are. I'd have arranged a meeting sooner."

"Really." Her chin went up a notch and her eyes

went flat. "I can't imagine why my looks matter."

"One can't help but appreciate beauty especially in the lowliest of places." Jason's smile stiffened at the edges. "I've recently become acquainted with Liam Gallagher. We're coordinating on a project together. He tells me you two were quite close once."

Her quick swallow was the only thing to give her away. She was tough and she was smart, but it was clear she didn't want to talk about Liam—whatever the hell his name was.

That made two of them. "Why don't we get to the reason you're here?"

Jason presented his back to Sophie. Dismissed her. "If we could speak privately for a moment?"

Sophie crossed her arms and settled farther into her chair. Other than lifting her bodily out of her seat there was no way he was going to get her to leave. So much for meeting with Jason in private. And for containment. These two had a history of being on opposite sides. Like lion and zebra they were both in it to win. Didn't mean he wanted Sophie on Jason's radar screen any more than necessary.

Caleb gestured toward the two stiff men standing off to the side. "Unfortunately, there's only room for one. Maybe your associates can find a seat at the bar?"

Sophie smirked. On Jason's signal the two oversized men, one hairy, one bald, ambled toward the front of the room.

Jason tapped his Rolex. "I'm expected for dinner at West in fifteen minutes."

"Yet you found the time to take a detour." Caleb shook his head as the waitress approached for Jason's order. "He's not staying."

Jason eyed Sophie and waited. When she remained seated he shifted to concentrate on Caleb. "I'm concerned certain people might be spreading nasty rumors about me."

"How tragic." Sophie stared at the side of Drummond's head hard enough to vaporize his brain. "Perhaps it would help if we knew who these people were?"

Jason raised a brow at Caleb. "Straight to the point. A quality I admire." He brushed at an imaginary speck on his lapel before turning to offer Sophie a small smile. "Here's to Caleb finally associating with a woman who has more to offer than a spray tan."

Jason Drummond was toying with his prey. But Caleb hadn't gotten to the top of his game by snapping at any old bait. Jason oozed arrogance, occupying as much space as possible. The faint derision he wore like spray cologne an offensive maneuver. Too bad his nerves showed in the occasional spin of his wedding ring. They'd played poker together enough times for Caleb to know his tell.

"I'm curious, what rumors are you talking about?"

Jason leaned back, draped one arm over the back of his chair. "Everyone wondered where you disappeared to Christmas Eve. Then over drinks at a Boxing Day party a mutual friend of ours mentioned seeing you at St. Paul's. He was on call and had to go in because of the storm. Apparently, both of you had your hands full."

Caleb shrugged. "I was approached by a third party who thought a young woman might need some legal advice."

Jason scoffed in Sophie's direction. "All part of the

service?"

The insult brought a rush of color to her cheeks. To her credit she didn't even flinch. She stared him down with equal amounts ice and fire. By not saying anything she said it all. Caleb fell a little bit in love.

Time for a dose of reality. "My client says you threatened her."

"Your client?" The look of disbelief on Jason's face wasn't feigned. Caleb couldn't stop the little rush of guilt. It didn't last long. Jason shifted in his chair, arms coming to rest on the table. "Yes, well, she also said she was on the pill."

"And what? You've never heard of condoms?" Sophie demanded.

"Sophie," warned Caleb. "Why don't you give us a minute?"

To his surprise she stood, her chair scraping along the floor. She added a mocking salute. "If you'll excuse me, I see a friend."

Jason waited until she was out of earshot before leaning in. "If she's a friend of Kellie's, I suggest you run in the opposite direction, my friend."

The use of Kellie's first name was a slap. He couldn't stop the stream of mental pictures, each one uglier than the last. "I can't discuss Ms. Andrews with you."

"And us being friends counts for nothing?" asked Jason.

This man was no friend of his. "You need to be having this discussion with your lawyer."

Jason moved closer, his voice low. "She worked on one of my projects. We hooked up a couple of times. Then one day she strolls into my office and announces she's pregnant. Wants to know what I'm going to do about it."

"So you're admitting to an affair?" Never mind his wife was a friend of Caleb's. "You should probably stop talking now."

Jason ignored him. "She said she needed money for an abortion. Her idea, not mine. I gave it to her, no questions asked. Which I thought was pretty damn sporting of me when there's no proof the kid's even mine. Imagine my surprise when a few months later she shows up at an event I happen to be attending with my wife."

"She says she was working the event." Caleb cursed himself for being stupid and opening his mouth. He knew better, was smarter, than this whole conversation.

"You don't know much about this neighborhood, do you? Golden Rule: Trust no one. Because here's a thought, maybe she's been playing me all along."

"And yet others suggest she's one in a long line." To hell with rules. Beer, body odor, and stale smoke clogged the air around them, but the man seated across from him made him gag. "She's eighteen years old and saying you left her pregnant and alone to fend for herself. Tell me I'm wrong."

"Watch yourself, Caleb." But Jason broke eye contact, only to recover a second later. "You don't want to go down this road."

"Are you threatening me?" They eyed each other. Eighteen years of passable friendship unraveled and reformed into something dark and menacing.

Jason straightened his shirt cuffs, the oversized diamond cufflinks winking in the harsh light. "Fact is the DTES is a dangerous place. Bad things happen here all the time." He signaled his men forward. "Spend enough time here and something bad is bound to happen to you."

They both stood. Jason Drummond could threaten him all he wanted. He wasn't worried for himself. Caleb put a restraining hand on Jason's arm. "If I find out you terrorized a young woman…"

Jason yanked his arm away and brushed off his sleeve. "We're friends so I'm going to choose not to take offence. But keep in mind I will not tolerate lies being spread about me. I felt it important to be upfront and honest. Feel free to pass the message on to any interested parties."

Jason Drummond's departure met with the same curious stares as his arrival. Sophie came to stand beside him. Caleb had zero time to compose himself. To fight against the instinct to say something stupid.

"Just stay calm and don't overreact. I'll handle this."

She crossed her arms. "Just what is it you think I'm going to do?"

Heads turned. He gritted his teeth. "I'm not going to apologize for wanting to protect Kellie. Or you."

"For real? You're going with the cave man approach? That's makes twice."

"Then throw me a raw steak and a club because I'm not sorry."

"This coming from the guy with the silver fork and knife set."

"Oh, for fu—, yes, I'm rich." He raised his voice. "Did you hear that in the back? Guilty as charged. Filthy stinking rich." He toughed out a smile and lifted a hand in recognition of the smattering of applause, the few catcalls. "It doesn't make me a bad guy."

Her anger flashed, then dissolved. Her teeth bit into her bottom lip, shutting down the beginning of a smile. "You're making a scene."

"Then let's take this outside."

"Fine." She sidestepped his tempt to touch her.

As a peace offering, he said. "If the public finds out about Quinn, he's ruined. He's going to do whatever he has to, to stop that from happening."

She nodded in agreement and just like that the fight was over. "And a man like Jason Drummond has the cash and connections to make his problems disappear."

"Yes, he does." No use pretending otherwise and she was too smart to fall for it. Jason Drummond would do whatever it took to protect his reputation, his political aspirations. He got a whiff of the orient and antiseptic before she put distance between them.

Her eyes narrowed to a squint. "He's not going to get away with it."

He couldn't decide if her mutinous expression turned him on or scared him to death. Truth was Jason Drummond came from a long line of men skilled at manipulation and getting their way. Their perch on the top of Vancouver's real estate pile hadn't come without claw marks.

"No, he's not. He's going to own up to his responsibilities." Caleb was careful to keep his expression impartial. Taking a stand never came cheap. He couldn't help wondering if any of them were prepared for the cost?

****

On the street the icy air did little to cool Sophie

down. Caleb showed no adverse effects at having Jason Drummond drop in on their *planning session*. Did nothing faze him? Or was he not invested enough to care? She inhaled hoping the chill would shock her system into neutral. So she could maintain a rational thought.

"I don't enjoy being dismissed." She paused while they both pulled out gloves and yanked coat collars up to their chins.

"Noted. Where are you parked?"

She pointed to a spot down the street. "What did Drummond say? Exactly."

And what, if anything, did Liam have to do with it?

He didn't shrug her question off, but met her look. She noted the concern darkening his eyes. Watched the jerk and tightening of his jaw. His decision, when he came to it, showed in the lowering of his brow. "He's setting himself up as the victim suggesting Kellie is playing him."

"Bastard. You've met her. You know that's ridiculous." She picked up her pace.

Caleb caught up. "Is it?"

"How can you ask that?" She stopped so fast he had to backtrack.

"I don't doubt Quinn is his biological son." A muscle jumped in his jaw as he searched her face. "But getting to the truth requires looking at this from all angles."

"Lucky me. Looks like I've got you for that."

"No, Kellie has me for that." He stepped in closer blocking out the street buzz. On a frosty cloud of breath he leaned in. "Who's Liam Gallagher?"

She blinked then swallowed. Neither helped.

"None of your business."

"It is if he's going to be a problem."

She snorted out a laugh. "Believe me, he's not."

"Then why would Jason mention him?"

It was a valid question. Because Liam had hurt her. Publicly humiliated her. Shattered her heart. But she'd moved on. What troubled her more was Liam's resentment of Marnie. He knew of her past struggles. He knew how much her sister meant to her and the lengths she'd go to keep her safe. "It doesn't matter. He doesn't matter."

"Forgive my skepticism."

Her heart skipped a beat, which was absurd. It wasn't jealousy darkening his eyes. It couldn't be. It was frustration. A man in blue work coveralls pushed past them and knocked her closer. Her gloved hands landed on Caleb's chest.

He was as enticing on the street as he'd been inside the Empress. More at ease and fitting in better then she'd thought possible. She tilted her head, raised a brow. "You're not going to make this a thing are you?"

"It's my job to lift the rocks and check underneath." He put his hands over hers holding them in place.

He had a killer smile. Not big or showy, but easy and natural. And those eyes. Intelligent and purposeful with enough wicked mixed in to make a woman wonder.

"There's nothing under this particular rock to interest you." Were her lids getting heavy? Her heart rate slowed down. His head dipped.

His lips touched down next to her ear. "Come home with me and I'll find out for myself."

She rolled her eyes. "You never give up."

He took her elbow. "Where are you parked?"

"Not happening, Caleb."

"Then I'll have to settle for walking you to your car."

Man, he was good at this seduction stuff. It was even working on her. She shook her head to clear it. "This way. Down from the Ovaltine Café."

They walked the last few feet in silence. In the darkening light she didn't notice anything wrong until they were almost there.

"Son of a bitch." Sophie marched up to her lopsided car. At the sight of slashed tires she spun around to face Caleb. He wasn't there, he was circling her vehicle. They made eye contact across the hood.

What she saw there set her back. Scraped raw of any charm, his face set in unforgiving lines, he was a different kind of animal.

"Come on." He rounded her car and reached for her elbow. "I'll take you home."

"Wait a minute." She hung back, fought to keep eye contact. "I have to phone and have it towed to a garage."

"I'll take care of it." He tightened his hold on her arm, tugged her along.

She stumbled after him for a second until she was able to dig in her heels. "Would you just give me a minute here?"

He stopped when she refused to move. "I said I'd take care of it and I will."

"Yeah, well, it's not your car. Ergo, it's not your job to *take care* of it."

"This isn't a conversation for the street." People

paused to stare or turned back to sneak a peek. A muscle jumped in his jaw when she neither budged nor answered.

"Fine." He pried the word out between stiff lips. "I'll drop you off at home and you can deal with it."

Apparently, he was under the misconception she'd been born yesterday. "So you can go after Jason Drummond. I don't think so."

"I don't have time for this." He stepped away. "Deal with your car however you like."

"Hold up there, Captain Marvel." She hustled after him. "What are you going to do? Challenge him to a duel? Come on. Let's take a moment and think this through."

He wasn't listening. He was pulling out his keys and unlocking the doors to his vehicle. She grabbed onto this arm.

"Caleb."

"Get in." He dragged his arm free and motioned to the passenger side.

"Okay." She held up a finger. "First. Stop ordering me around. I don't like it. Second. You're not thinking straight. That's going to lead to a mistake."

"No. It's not." He made his way around to the driver's side, opened the door, jumped in and slammed it shut.

She gritted her teeth, forced to scramble into the passenger seat before he put it in gear. "We don't know for sure it was Drummond."

His eyes on the rear-view mirror he checked traffic. "Then I'll have to ask him."

"Don't get stupid on me, Caleb." She clicked her seatbelt into place.

He spared her a glance before pulling out onto Hastings Street. "Excuse me for wanting to plant a fist in the face of the man who threatened you."

She blinked at the possessiveness of his statement. His white knight act caused little flares of heat to ignite along her nerve endings. A small smile slipped out before she shut it down. "Look, I appreciate the concern. But I don't think resorting to assault and battery is the best course of action."

"Then you aren't sitting where I'm sitting."

He was gripping the gearshift. She put a hand over his. "Take me home. I'll cook you dinner. We'll talk."

He kept his eyes on the road. "Tempting, but no."

She should let them duke it out over canapés.

"Please." The word stumbled out of her mouth tasting of frustration proving pleading wasn't her thing.

He pulled his hand out from under hers. "I can't."

"Yes, you can. You absolutely can." She nudged him with her elbow. "Because I've got this extra expensive can of soup I've been saving for a special occasion."

He snorted out a laugh, then sobered. "This isn't funny."

"I know." She fixated on the traffic light about to turn red and gripped the armrest. "But I don't want to have to worry about you too."

He hit the brake, shifted in his seat after skidding to a stop. "I'm not letting this go."

"No. But maybe we can come up with a smarter plan than storming one of Vancouver's most upscale restaurants."

"You eat canned soup. I'm in the mood for pretentious."

"Then I'll serve with it with the expensive Saltines."

He stared straight ahead. "He's going to pay for this."

"Absolutely."

"We're ordering in. I'm buying. No arguing."

"If you say so. Although it is gourmet chicken noodle so you may want to rethink." Oh crackers, was she flirting? Hard to know since she'd never done it before.

His lips lifted.

"That's better." But she still needed to clarify a few things. Make him understand. "Don't make me the reason you go after Drummond. I don't want that. I don't need that. What I want is Kellie and Quinn safe. Use them as your motivation. Not me."

He ran a hand through his hair sending all those lovely dark strands poking out in different directions. She'd never seen him looking anything less than immaculate. Even after helping deliver a baby. This side of him was more interesting, more three-dimensional. Less charm more intensity.

"While we're clarifying matters, know this." He found her hand with his and threaded his fingers through hers. She didn't resist the urge to twine her fingers with his. "You matter to me."

His grip tightened when she tried to pull free. She let him have his way. Didn't try very hard to dislodge him. "Let's not get all sappy."

"Is this what you're like in bed? Practical with a little no-nonsense added in." The light turned green and they were moving again.

She kept her mouth shut.

"Because I like it." His grin had the power to scatter her common sense.

She tried to stem the blush heating up her skin. Didn't succeed. "The jury's still out on whether you'll get the chance to find out."

He settled back into his seat. "But I haven't had a chance to present my closing arguments and I usually rock that part."

"I'll bet." She copped a peek, made note of his curved lips and rolled her eyes.

They rode the rest of the way in silence, each lost in thought. He wasn't going to let any of it go, not Jason's intrusion, not her tires, not Liam. Sooner or later he was going to ask again. She was going to have to decide what to tell him.

***

Caleb held the front door of her street level apartment open hoping they'd find a little time to spend alone. They walked into chaos. Quinn was wailing. How something so small could make so much noise was confounding. But Quinn wasn't the only one in tears. So was Kellie. Marnie rushed them the minute they stepped through the door, phone to her ear, cigarette dangling from between her stained fingers.

"Where the hell have you been? And why aren't you answering your cell?" She stuffed her phone away in a pocket. Ashes spilled from the tip of her cigarette to the floor. When she spotted Caleb she pointed it at him. "What's he doing here? Does he live here now or something?"

Kellie pushed past Marnie tears streaming down her face. "He won't stop crying. I think he's sick."

Sophie shrugged out of her coat and passed it to

Caleb. "Here let's check things out."

Kellie sniffed and hugged Quinn close. "He's fed, changed, but he won't sleep and all he does is cry."

Sophie made her way into the living room and held out her arms for Quinn. "I'm pretty sure he's fine. Just a little unhappy at the moment. Caleb, pass me the blanket from the back of the couch."

She wrapped the baby up tight and signaled for Caleb to come closer like she was preparing to dump the screaming bundle of demon baby on him. He backed up. "No. No way."

She came to him and literally shoved Quinn at him. "Like this." She positioned one of his hands under the baby's head and the other one under his tiny butt.

"It's not working." If anything he got louder.

"Give it a second. Come on, bring him in closer. Cradle him." She nodded as he adjusted. "Just like that. In the crook of your arm with your other arm here. Easy peasy. Kellie, come with me."

"Wait." *What?* Quinn, as panicked as Caleb, increased his bawling. "Where are you going?"

"I'm taking Kellie. I'm going to run her a bath." She motioned to Kellie who didn't seem to want to leave Quinn with Caleb any more than Caleb wanted to be left. Finally, Sophie pulled her in the direction of the bathroom. "He'll be fine. She needs a break. So do I. We're taking ten."

Caleb looked down at Quinn who was screaming, eyes closed tight. Caleb bobbed up and down.

"Really? You think bouncing is going to help?" Marnie brushed past him. "Like we haven't been doing that for the last two hours."

No one was more surprised than Caleb when Quinn

quieted down a decibel. He added a rocking motion and Quinn dialed it back some more. Then it was no more than a whimper. Maybe this wasn't so hard after all. He shot Marnie a smug smile.

"Ah, jeez. Men. Days old and they know to stick together." She stabbed out her smoke in an overflowing ashtray. "But at least he's quiet."

"Now what should I do?"

"Why don't we pause for a moment while I consult my ovaries?" She sneered at him. "I don't know. Keep walking. Read him the sports section. Lactate. Do whatever it takes as long as the result is silence." She placed a hand over her forehead and closed her eyes.

He paced. The kid was kind of cute when he wasn't beet red. Caleb froze when Quinn screwed up his face and opened his mouth.

"What is it?" demanded Marnie.

Caleb relaxed when it turned into a yawn. "Nothing. False alarm."

"Thank God. I can't take anymore crying." Marnie moved to stand in front of the picture window overlooking the street. She frowned, searching the dark. "Where's Sophie's car?"

Caleb went on alert, not knowing how much Sophie wanted her to know. He shrugged, kept his head down and his gaze on Quinn. "Tire trouble."

"Shit." Marnie shook her head and turned back to the window. "She'll probably walk to work tomorrow. In the dark. I hate it when she goes out in the dark. She thinks she's immune to all the crap going on around here."

Surprised, Caleb lifted his head to stare at her back. Somehow Marnie had found a way to keep track of her little sister without Sophie knowing it. "If you take Quinn, I can phone someone to take care of it and have her car back here before she needs to leave for work tomorrow."

Her eyes lifted to watch him in the black of the window. A second later she turned and held out her arms. "Fine."

Caleb handed over Quinn and dug out his cell phone. Out of earshot in the kitchen, he made arrangements. When he was done he turned to head back into the living room and almost ran into Marnie.

She was still holding Quinn. Her voice low and softer then he'd ever heard it. "What kind of tire trouble did you say it was?"

Caleb pursed his lips. He didn't break eye contact and neither did she. "I didn't."

She opened her mouth, then shut it. Quinn squirmed in her arms. Caleb backed up because he'd seen that look before, in Sophie's eyes right before she'd dumped Quinn on him. Marnie glared at him. "He wants his Daddy back."

"If the shoe fits…" Caleb backed up another step.

"Asshole." But it was missing any serious heat.

Caleb countered. "I'll tell you if you do me a favor?"

"She's my sister. If something's happened I want to know."

Caleb stood silent and waited.

Marnie advanced, baby and all. Her voice was still low, but her eyes flashed fanatical fire. "I protect what's mine."

He went with his gut. "You care about her."

"Of course, I care about her." The long line of her

scar contracted as her jaw tightened. "She's my sister."

"Pretty standard line. Could mean everything or nothing."

Marnie stared at him. "What's the favor?"

Caleb had a clear line down the hall. No sign of Sophie. "I need you to stay here tonight and I need you to stay…alert. Call the police first and me second if anything happens or you think something is going to happen."

Her eyes glittered. "What happened to Sophie's car?"

"Someone slashed her tires outside the Empress."

"Someone?" And once again his arms where full of baby. Marnie paced out of the room and back in again. "What were you doing at the Empress? She shouldn't be at the Empress. She shouldn't be anywhere near this hell hole of a place at all."

Interesting.

Caleb added, "We stopped in to have a drink."

Marnie mocked, "I'm guessing the drink was your idea and the Empress was Sophie's?"

He neither confirmed nor denied. "Jason Drummond happened to stop in while we were there."

He had to look twice, but he was positive it was relief he saw in her eyes. "Wait a minute, who were you expecting—"

"That son of a bitch." She headed in the direction of the front door and Caleb scrambled after her Quinn half asleep in his arms. His gaze landed on the little temporary crib set up in the corner. As gently as possible, as quickly as possible, he settled Quinn in it. "Where do you think you're going?"

"Out."

"No, you're not. You're staying here."

"You stay here. Play watchdog or whatever. I've got things to do."

"No, you don't."

"Look at the bright side. Here's your chance to have a sleepover."

"Nice."

"What? I'm supposed to be ignorant of the fact you're trying to bang my sister?"

"You have a real way with words, you know that?"

"Whatever."

"Sit down. Now."

"Or what?"

"Sophie's not ready to let me stay here. You'll be leaving them unprotected. Vulnerable. Is that your idea of looking after your own?"

"Fine." She stormed over to the couch and plopped down. "We'll all sit around watch Oprah reruns and wait for our periods to sync."

"That's the spirit. For the record, I respect the hell out of your sister. I not looking to take advantage of the situation nor am I helping her in the hopes it will lead to more."

"Did I ask you your intentions?" She settled back against the couch. She propped an ankle over her knee.

"I need to know I can count on you."

"Count on her for what?" asked Sophie. He glanced over his shoulder to see her standing there, arms crossed, brows raised, and her hip cocked.

Before Caleb could open his mouth, Marnie snorted and opened hers. "To babysit you tonight."

"Really?" Sophie uncrossed her arms and came to stand between him and her sister. "I'm getting damn tired of having this conversation."

Caleb rubbed a hand over his throbbing forehead before stabbing a finger in each of their directions. "The two of you? You're more alike than you know. I only thought with Kellie and Quinn here and after what happened earlier you'd appreciate the extra security. An extra set of eyes."

"And as much as it pains me to say this: He's right." Marnie made eye contact and her promise to him was in the hard glint of her eyes. "So, I'll be staying."

He nodded his thanks. "Great. So, how about some dinner? Chinese or Pizza?"

Sophie put her hand out. "Not so fast. You may think you've dodged a bullet, but keep this in mind."

He'd do anything to see she didn't get hurt. Caleb reached up and when she didn't back away he smoothed a thumb over her cheek. "I'm waiting."

"You're lucky I'm starving."

Marnie smirked out a laugh.

Lucky didn't begin to cover it. He listened to them quibble over what to order. He might have a handle on things tonight. Jason was unlikely to do anything else, satisfied with his warning. But tomorrow was a whole new day and he had some threats of his own to make.

****

Sophie sat cross-legged on the couch, Quinn tucked in front of her, Kellie in the shower, Marnie out. A truce called, at least for the time being. She leaned in and tickled Quinn's tummy. So sweet, swaddled in a blanket, his innocence a reminder of how they all started out.

Her clinic was open half-days on Friday, the afternoon meant for paperwork and debriefing with her staff. To avoid burnout they gathered to rehash the week's challenges and share victories. They tried very hard not to take their work home with them. Even Sophie. Her work had consumed her at the beginning. But after Liam left she'd reevaluated.

Somewhat.

She wrapped Quinn's tiny fingers around one of hers. But this afternoon the rest of her staff were on their own. Sophie was at home. The clinic the least of her worries, Marnie her biggest, Jason Drummond a close second. Then there was Kellie and Quinn.

"Who could resist fussing over you? With your ten tiny fingers and ten tiny toes."

And Caleb.

It was dangerous to think of Caleb while playing with Quinn. Not the best way to keep things casual. Tying her want of a family to him. Hard not to do when he arranged for tow trucks, gifts, and helped deliver midnight babies on Christmas Eve. His armor might be Armani, but he continued to prove he could take a hit.

Quinn's cheek was soft under her fingertip. She cooed at him. His little mouth opened wide and he yawned in response. It was enough to toast her marshmallow of a heart. She refused to apologize for wanting a baby in her womb. Or a man worthy of her yearnings. And screw anyone brave enough to judge.

She thought she'd found it once, her happily-ever-after. Then Liam had found Charity Owens, dog walker. They'd sent her a birth announcement twenty-one months later. Not to be mean. The announcement had gone out as a mass email, hers included. By mistake, she was sure. Neither of them smart enough to do it on purpose.

That's right.

Meow.

Now her ovaries were thirty-two years old. Her finite number of eggs was dwindling. She'd always pictured kids in her future. Lots of them. Wanting to do the right thing, knowing she must, hadn't stemmed those dreams.

Not at all.

She shook the maudlin thoughts off. She couldn't afford to go there. Not when she had this little one and his mother to protect. She didn't want Quinn's life to be a battle for survival. His little arms flailed like he sensed her mood. He let out a whimper. She scooped him up and cuddled him close. Who could resist inhaling the scent of him? He was a tiny bundle of baby crack.

"You are so yummy. I could eat you up. Yes, I could. Beautiful boy." She sang. She rocked. Then stopped. Thought, oh shit.

In over my head.

She was falling for two different guys and they both had bad idea written all over them. One was spoken for and the other one came with an expiration date. Choices. She settled back with a drowsy Quinn. Like she didn't have her hands full with Marnie.

Kellie wondered back into the room. Pretty in a mint green T-shirt she was looking better every day, more color in her cheeks, less hollow. Sophie had lent her some clothes, but they were going to have to go shopping. With her hair in a ponytail, blue eyes alert, and her smile a little hesitant she sat down across from Sophie.

"I can take him if you want?"

"I don't mind." Sophie smiled at her, hoping to reassure. Kellie didn't like to let Quinn out of her sight. Sophie understood her terror at losing him.

Which meant they needed to talk about the elephant in the room. Or the herd of elephants. "Kellie, I need to ask if there's something you haven't told me? About Marnie? About Jason Drummond?"

The timid smile disappeared. She folded her arms across her stomach like all of a sudden it ached. "I've told you everything."

"I know it was Marnie who introduced you to Drummond." It hurt so bad to go there. To know her sister pimped out girls like Kellie to a creep like Jason Drummond.

"She didn't mean any harm." Kellie jerked forward to perch at the very end of her seat. "We didn't plan any of this. We didn't. Please, don't blame her."

How could she not? "I believe you about the pregnancy. But are you sure there's not something you're leaving out. If Marnie is pushing—"

"No. She's trying to protect us from him."

She didn't doubt it was true. The knowledge kept her up at night. "You have to know she's in no shape to protect anyone. She's ill, Kellie."

"We'll be fine." She shifted, looked away. It was a lie. The last thing they were was fine and Kellie knew it.

"No, you won't. As long as Marnie's not thinking straight and you're listening to her, things are going to get worse."

"You're wrong."

"No, I'm not. She's my sister. I know her. I know her history."

107

"Yeah, I know." For the first time condemnation harshened her words. "She told me all about *her family*. She told me everything. About how your parents kicked her out with nothing. They didn't love her. They didn't want her around. I know what that feels like, I understand her."

Whereas Sophie never would because she'd been wanted, cherished. Protected.

Not her fault.

And it was time to let it go.

"Kellie, you're only eighteen years old. Someone is supposed to be looking after you."

"In birth years, not street years. I know she's in trouble. I know she needs help. I'm not stupid. But I don't want to lose her too."

"You won't lose her. She loves you. But you can love her back and still do what you know is best for you and Quinn."

"I don't want to be disloyal to Marnie." Her sigh was soft, a puff of breath, then another, and another. She breathed deep, swallowed. "But...you've been so great to me. Caleb too. It's so nice here. Calm. Clean. I can think straight here."

Sophie put a hand on Kellie's knee and squeezed. "Knowing what you want is nothing to apologize for. It's a good thing. A good start."

Kellie sniffed and grabbed a tissue from the box to wipe her nose and stop the tears. "I do want calm for Quinn. But I don't know how to make it happen without hurting Marnie."

"We'll figure out a way. I promise. I'm here to help. So is Caleb. You can tell us anything and it will remain in confidence."

Kellie's eyes were full of the same thing she saw at night in the mirror. Loyalty. Love. Futility. "I want her to be okay."

"So do I."

She straightened her shoulders, stuck out her chin, her knuckles white. "And I'm not letting that sick bastard touch my kid. I don't care what I have to do. Or say. It's not happening."

Sophie nodded and gave her knee another squeeze. She didn't want to make promises she couldn't keep. David didn't always win. She was terrified this time life was going to swing in favor of Goliath.

****

Caleb had a thing about tyrants. He imagined most people did. He planned on making those feelings very clear to Jason Drummond. Playing by the rules wasn't on the agenda. He walked in knowing the score. He'd weighed the possible cost to his career in coming, allowed for his growing feelings for Sophie. But in the end the future of a young mother and her tiny baby made his decision, and doing the wrong thing for the right reason, easy.

He charged past the receptionist and pushed his way into Jason's ultramodern private office. Steel and glass. Sixteen stories off the pavement in the Shaw Tower where the Drummond Group owned an entire floor.

"Caleb." Jason Drummond tapped his keyboard and sat back in his chair. Superior smeared across his face. Hell, it was woven into the fabric of his suit. A scent in the air. "What a surprise."

"I doubt it." He wouldn't have gotten this far if Jason had wanted to keep him out. He straightened the sleeves of his own suit. Jason wasn't the only one accomplished at aloof. Trained in the art of getting your own way. Expecting it.

"You wound me, Caleb. You really do." He steepled his fingers, tapped them against his chin. "My door is always open to you."

"A bill. For Dr. Monroe's tires." He tossed an envelope onto Jason's desk. They weren't alone in his chrome-plated tower. The hairy goon from the night before was with him. The other hustled in through the open door. Caleb barely spared them a glance.

"It's all right, gentlemen, no threat here. You can leave." Jason waved them off. They backed out of the room with heavy frowns and gritted teeth. Jason picked up the envelope, set it aside. "Let me pour you a drink. You look like you could use one."

"No, thanks." Jason got up and poured himself a couple of fingers of expensive scotch. Caleb remembered a time when he'd been impressed by the man's easy confidence. Not anymore. "I'll make this simple. You stay away from Dr. Monroe and her clinic. You stay away from my client and anyone involved with her. Are we clear?"

Jason adopted a look of confusion. "I seem to be missing something as I can assure you I want nothing to do with your client. Or the good doctor."

"You're intimidation tactics aren't going to work."

Another sip of scotch. Another brief smile. "Are you accusing me of something?"

Damn right he was. "Just making sure we both know the stakes."

"You want to get a handle on the stakes? I care about this city. I'm willing to take it to the next level.

We're ready. The 2010 Olympics proved it. I can make it happen."

Like his glass office, it was all about the show. "No matter who gets in your way?"

The other man ignored him. "This is bigger than any of that. Cleaning up the DTES is a huge part of the plan. Surely, after spending the last few days there you agree with me."

"The plan?" Caleb didn't know about a plan but he sure as hell was looking at the problem.

"Facts are facts." Jason slung his arm across Caleb's shoulders. It was an old familiar gesture of camaraderie. It took everything Caleb had not to shrug him off. To not give too much away. "The Downtown Eastside is an embarrassment."

Drummond pointed to small table holding a 3-D model of an altered DTES. "That's tomorrow's reality. A revitalization plan benefitting the whole city. Work with me, Caleb. Join my campaign team and we can take this city to the next level. A global level."

Join his—Caleb stepped away. "What about the people already living in the Downtown Eastside? How does your grand plan affect their community?"

"What community? Jesus Christ, Caleb, they're talking about doling out liquor to the hard-core cases. Like ghetto-style missions and supervised safe injection sites aren't bad enough? We need to draw the line."

"You're trying to gentrify the neighborhood. Push out people who have nowhere else to go."

"Listen to yourself. When did you become a crusader for the downtrodden? With your taste for expensive cars, not to mention women, and your place in Yaletown."

"After an addict lands in a neighborhood like the DTES, what do you think comes next?"

Drummond shrugged his shoulders like it wasn't any of his concern. "How the hell should I know?"

"There is no next, Jason," Caleb said. "There's nowhere else to go. Nowhere to push them. This is the end of the line. Instead of luxury condos why not more low-income housing?"

"She's getting to you, isn't she? Too much thinking with your dick, my man. What do you think? Million-dollar condos are going to appear on the corner of Main and Hastings overnight?" He slapped a hand on Caleb's shoulder, like he'd done many times in the past. Only this time the laughter was forced, uncomfortable. "Look, a lot has to happen before all roads leading to the DTES are paved with caramel macchiatos."

"And while you're out there playing the hardline advocate, the Drummond Group is buying up all the lovely, cheap property available in the Downtown Eastside."

Jason didn't deny it, but the warning was in his eyes and the thin line of his mouth.

"I checked." Caleb strolled over to the miniature model, tapped the top of a teeny tiny building, and whistled. "Imagine my surprise at learning how much property you own down there. And how much you stand to make on this revitalization project of yours."

A telltale red flush stained Jason's cheeks. He gave his wedding ring a twist. "I'd be very interested in knowing how you came by your information."

"It's amazing what one learns when one knows how and who to ask." Caleb turned the knife. "You're not the only one with connections."

Jason shrugged. "Acquisitions are kind of what I do as managing director of corporate development."

Caleb made a cursory glance of the glossy office then he nodded. "True, but I was referring more to your personal portfolio."

Jason offered a lot more teeth and grit than smile. "Be careful where you go with this, Caleb."

Caleb got in his face. "I'll go anywhere I like. Do whatever it takes to protect an eighteen-year-old girl from the likes of you. Not only that, I'm going to make sure it doesn't happen again, with another girl too alone, too broke, and too desperate to say no. That means I'm going to start by finding out who your pimp is. Or you could make it easy and tell me who supplies the girls?"

"I don't know what you're talking about." Jason threw back the rest of his scotch. "But word of warning, I'd be careful while turning over all those stones. There's no putting them back and covering up what you didn't want to know."

"Who *arranged* for you to meet Kellie?"

Jason didn't move. "I thought we had an understanding."

"And your son?"

"Don't push me."

Caleb changed tactics. "She's terrified of you."

"An unfortunate misunderstanding, I'm sure."

He wanted to keep him off center enough to make a mistake. "So you're going to forget you have a son?"

"What would you have me do? On second thought, don't answer that." He made his way back to the bottle of scotch, poured another couple of fingers, tossed back a mouthful.

"You could step up? Do the right thing. Be the kind of dad your father never was."

"In return, I lose my wife, not to mention all her lovely money, my reputation, and the chance to lead this city into a very promising future. It's not the way I see things playing out. So you can tell her to keep her kid away from me and to call off her pit bull."

Pit bull? Caleb focused in on Jason, on his white knuckled handling of his glass, his tight jaw. To keep his own hands from betraying his confusion he shoved them in his pants pocket. "What are you talking about?"

"I'm talking about extortion." His lip curled. "She came to my house, Caleb. My house."

Caleb gritted his teeth. "Explain."

Jason lifted his glass in triumph. His anger melted away, like the ice in his glass, warmed by the elixir of having the upper hand. "Ah, I see she left that part out. How convenient. Well, here's a message from me: Tell the little mother if she wants money she's going to have to deal with me directly. I won't tolerate being blackmailed. Once I'm sure without a shadow of doubt the child is mine I'm more than willing to pay a reasonable amount of child support. On the condition I never have to see or hear from her or her son again. Ever. Do we understand each other?"

Caleb gave a short nod, his eyes preferring the view from the vast expanse of windows to his left than the sight of the man standing in front of him.

"Make this go away." It was a demand spoken and delivered by a man expecting nothing less than subservience. "And it'll be over."

Anger, futile and counterproductive, seduced him. Heated his skin. It stroked and suggested. It taunted him to lash out. He kept it to himself, to serve up later. "I'll be sure to relay your generous offer."

"And Caleb? If the news of my…indiscretion leaks to the public, I'll have no choice but to have her declared unfit and have her child taken away. Then I'm coming after you and the good doctor and when I'm done with you there won't be anything left."

Caleb pulled another envelope out of the inside pocket of his suit jacket and tossed it on the desk. "You require paternity testing be done? Here's where you need to go. The sooner you make an appointment, the sooner we can get this over with."

The door to his office opened, and one of men who'd accompanied Jason to the Empress stepped in and crossed his arms. Rage curled into a ball in his belly. He refused to let it take over. Fought to stay calm so his next words would have the maximum effect. "Know this, if anything happens to Dr. Monroe or Kellie Andrews, no amount of money or powerful family connections will save you from me."

"An inflated sense of power is a dangerous thing. Warning, forget about my personal business and stop prying into things that are none of your concern. You're standing on quicksand, Caleb. Sooner or later it's going to pull you under."

Caleb let him have the last word. He walked out without looking back. It didn't matter. Nothing was going to protect any of them from a wildcard like Marnie, because it sure as hell hadn't been Kellie making blackmail demands.

****

Sophie opened the door to Caleb. There was no stopping the rush at seeing him. Or the relief. Marnie was back and ready to climb the walls. It had taken all Sophie had to keep her halfway calm. He loosened his tie and stalked past her into the living room.

Okay.

Now what?

Sophie dogged after him knowing she didn't want to hear it. His anger a wave sweeping across the whole room until his gaze crashed with her sister's.

"What the hell were you thinking?" he demanded.

Sophie stepped in front of him. "What's wrong?"

He shot his answer over her shoulder at Marnie. "You went to see him. At his house."

"So what?"

He pushed past her ready to do battle. "You're blackmailing him."

Marnie rounded on Caleb, a fight in her eyes. "He deserves to pay."

Sophie closed her eyes. No. She wouldn't be so careless. Except Marnie wouldn't see it as reckless, worse dangerous. She was trying to help a friend.

Caleb turned his attention to a cringing Kellie. "Did you know about this?"

Sophie caught the glare Marnie shot at Kellie. Kellie's arms tightened around Quinn and he squirmed in protest. Still looking, her eyes wide and disbelieving, at Marnie, she shook her head.

"And what did you think it was going to accomplish except make him furious?" he ground out.

Marnie advanced. "He deserves to pay."

Sophie put a hand on her sister's arm to stop her from going any further. Marnie yanked out of her grasp eyes still on Caleb. Inside she seethed, on the surface she tried for zen. "I know you were trying to help. But we have to stick to the plan. For everyone's sake."

"And how much of the money made it into Kellie's hands and how much of it did you shoot into your arm?"

"Caleb, calm down." It was a legitimate question, but this wasn't the way to get answers from Marnie. Demands and accusations always backfired and the consolation rush of getting angry didn't last long enough to make it worthwhile. "There's a better way to do this."

But he wasn't done. He was past listening. "You're the doctor, how can you *not* tell she's using?"

It hurt. The truth and his tone. And the fact she was stuck as the monkey in the middle trying to catch the blame ball. "There's this little thing called doctor-patient privilege. You might have heard of it in your line of work?"

He ignored her and gestured at Marnie. "Push up your sleeves."

Okay, not so much a discussion as a full-on fight.

"Go to hell." She tried to push past, but Caleb blocked her way. Marnie was vibrating with a kitchen sink's worth of emotions. It was impossible to get a read and deflect the most pressing ones.

He spread his arms out wide in invitation. "After you."

"I'm out of here."

"You're not going anywhere until you hear what I have to stay." He stepped in front of her again as Marnie made another charge for the door. It left them nose to nose. Marnie stepped back first. "Stay away from Jason Drummond. You're backing him into a corner. He's not done making threats. Ones he can make good on. If you keep at him, he's going to take his son away from her."

Kellie gasped. "What?"

"Yeah, right." But Marnie raised a shaking hand to her forehead and rubbed at her hairline.

"Who do you think the judge is going to award custody to, huh? A pillar of the community looking out for his son's best interest no matter the personal cost to himself? Or a young woman with no job, no prospects, who's current address is an SRO at the Balmoral? Oh wait, her junkie of a best friend can vouch for her. Because that's how he's going to spin it. And Jason's not going to stop there, he'll go after Sophie. Is that what you want? IS IT?"

"I take care of my own."

"Bullshit." He stabbed a finger in Marnie's direction. "You need help and the sooner you get it the better. Because right now you can't even take care of yourself."

"I'm getting damn sick and tired of hearing people say that." Marnie slammed past him and grabbed her coat on her way out the door.

The crash and echoing silence was suffocating.

Sophie pushed back her hair. Her head ached. Her body too. "I take it you went to see Drummond?"

Kellie stood up clutching Quinn to her, eyes wide and terrorized. "Is that what he's going to do? Sue for custody? Am I going to lose Quinn?"

"Of course not." Sophie hugged her tight. She put a shitload of warning into her next words. "Right, Caleb?"

Caleb's laugh lacked any amusement. He scrubbed a hand over his face. "Don't worry. The last thing he wants is to harm his reputation. But no one wants to be vulnerable to a blackmailer and someone with Jason's massive ego is going to push back. The good news is he's agreed to talk about child support. But, Kellie, you need to be aware any money paid to you is for you and Quinn. Understood?"

She nodded, but Sophie noticed she avoided eye contact. Seconds later she escaped with Quinn into her temporary bedroom.

"You certainly know how to clear a room." Sophie dropped down onto the couch and grabbed a pillow to hug.

"You're still here." It fell somewhere between a question and a statement.

"Yeah, well, it is my house."

"Do you want me to leave?"

She knew he'd walk back out her door if she wanted him to, but she didn't. She didn't want to be a lone with this mess. "I want you to explain what happened in your meeting."

"She went to his house demanding money." He chose the stuffed chair across from her. His elbows landed on his thighs, his hands coming together to support his chin. He shook his head like he still couldn't believe she'd done it.

"I wish I could predict what she's going to do next." She left out any mention of the knife incident for now. "One minute she wants him involved, the next not at all. It's not an excuse, it's an insight to how her mind works. With us involved she has less control over things and the harder she's going to work to get it back."

"Do you think it was the drugs talking?"

"Partly, but it's also a symptom of her mental illness. We worked so hard on her recovery." She closed her eyes in defeat, let her body sag back against the cushions. "I knew. I didn't want to believe it."

The couch dipped and strong hands came to rest on either side of her face. "Hey, she makes her own choices."

"I know. I just want her to be different. To be all right."

He gathered her up. She rested her head against his chest, let his heartbeat lull her. "I know. Maybe treatment?"

"I've tried, but she won't go." She glanced up at him. "But you're thinking treatment would solve more than one problem, aren't you?"

He ran a hand over her hair. "I'm not going to lie. Marnie safely out of our way would solve a lot of problems. Jason might even sink to being reasonable."

"I'm not going to push her in a direction because it's convenient to our cause. Right now, she's completely resistant to the idea. She won't abandon Kellie."

"She's not helping her. She's making things worse."

"It's twisted I know. Are you going to tell me the rest of what happened with Jason?"

"There was nothing else."

"Caleb. Don't start lying now. Did he threaten you?"

"I'm not worried about me."

"Meaning he threatened me." She swallowed the overwhelming urge to sigh.

"I'm not going to let anything happen to you." His

knuckles were gentle against her cheek.

"That makes two of us, because I'm not going to let anything happen to me either."

"There's nothing more we can do tonight." His whisper brushed against her ear. A second later his lips touched the sensitive spot below it. "Unless you're willing to come home with me? We could take a few hours. Forget this whole mess existed."

A great prescription for a little stress relief. And just what the doctor needed.

****

Sophie stood up and held out her hand. His exaggerated sigh made her smile. When he was on his feet, she stepped in closer and slipped the knot free on his tie. Her heartbeat echoed in her ears. His tie drifted to the floor. She undid the first button of his shirt. Trailed a finger over the pulse beating at the base of his neck.

He put a hand over hers. "Just so we're clear, one more button and I'm here for the night."

"Just so we're clear?" She looked up at him through her lashes. "That's my goal."

His Adam's apple bobbed. "I think I can work within the parameters of your goal."

She put a finger against his lips. "How about a little less talk."

His hand clutched at the back of her head. He bent down and stopped a couple of heartbeats short of her mouth. Her finger was still pressed against his lips. He drew it into his mouth and held it between his teeth. She saw it in his eyes before she felt it on her skin. His bite. His tongue lapped away the sting. Suction. Every ounce of want went nuclear. She dislodged her finger so she could twist her fingers into his hair, her other hand went for his belt.

With his mouth engaged, his hands went every direction. He invaded her space, backed her up, herded her in the direction of her bedroom. His tongue dominated her mouth, tasting and taking. She gave up trying to undo his pants and held on. Her fingers digging into muscles she forgot the names of as she kissed him back. When the back of her knees hit the end of her bed she breathed a sigh of relief.

Yes.

They landed on the bed in a puff of covers. He shifted in the dark and turned on her bedside lamp. In the soft glow he pulled a condom out of his wallet and set it down on her nightstand. Then he came for her. He ran his hands through the short strands of her hair while his mouth learned the shape of hers. Over her, pressing her into the plump duvet. The heat was incredible. It burned away the chaos of the last few days, the worry and uncertainty. She let them go. He was right. Their troubles could wait a few hours.

She needed this. More, she needed him. The thought didn't scare her. It put her back on track with his belt and getting his pants down. Her shirt came off followed by her bra. Under the heat of his mouth and the scrape of his tongue, her body tightened even as it stretched. This was a good decision. Because of the man she'd chosen.

"You are so beautiful." His words drifted over her skin on puffs of breath. He backed them up with actions. As her panties slipped down her legs and her thighs opened he said them again. His tongue mapped a route to the place she ached for him to find. She didn't need to hold him there, his hands clamped onto her thighs. He concentrated his attentions between her legs until she died trying to hold it all inside.

She let go on a skydive of feeling so intense she rode it all the way to absolution. Only to have it build again as he made his way back up her body. Her eyes drifted closed.

"Oh, no, you don't. Eyes open."

With his mouth on hers he shifted his weight to the side. She lifted her head to watch him reach for the package he'd placed next to her alarm clock. When their eyes met she reached between their bodies and stroked. He lowered his forehead to hers. His rasps of breath warm against her cheek.

"That feels so good."

Her hand tightened around him and his whole body shuddered in readiness.

He ripped open the package and pulled her hand away. In its place went the condom. Their lips met as he pushed into her. His forearms came to rest on either side of her head. Her hands ran over his broad shoulders, across damp skin and taut muscle. Everything about him was hard. Everything in her opened. Until the moment came and it stretched leaving them both gasping, holding on, riding it out.

Her heart continued to pound after he rolled off and she felt the bed dip. She risked opening an eye. A naked Caleb stole a look-see down the hall before making his way to the bathroom. The brief glow of the bathroom light flicking on and then darkness.

She scrambled to get underneath the sexed up covers, pulling them up to her chin. The bathroom door opened and she stopped breathing, which was ridiculous. She was an adult, with adult needs. And one of those needs was sex. Obviously.

Because it was true she flipped back the covers on his side of the bed in blatant invitation.

Trust Caleb not to disappoint. He crawled into to bed like the spot already recognized his shape.

"You smell like sin." His whisper followed the path of her collarbone. He might as well have been speaking directly to her vagina.

But one of them had to be practical so she said, "I do not."

Did she?

Crap. She was losing her mind.

His warm hand cupped one breast and gifted kisses on the other. She melted like milk chocolate. Her hand burrowed into his hair. The fingers of her other hand skimmed the line of his shoulders, swirled circles over his skin.

"Caleb." It was a warning. Sort of. Her breathing was a little sketchy at the moment.

"Sophie." He traced circles around her peaked nipple.

Again with the practical. "How many condoms do you carry around with you?"

He smiled against her breast. She felt the brush of his lashes. "How many do you?"

"None."

It stopped him in his tracks. He looked her in the eye. "None? At all?"

She shook her head. She couldn't remember the last time she even gave needing a supply a thought.

"Birth control pill?"

"Yes."

"Thank God."

"I don't know you well enough for unprotected sex, Caleb."

"Trust me. I would never do anything to put your life at risk. I'm clean. I promise."

"I'm going to need to see proof."

His eyebrows lifted. "What?"

"Exactly what I said. Do you have any idea how many cases of HIV and AIDS I deal with every week in my practice? Not to mention STD's?"

He sat up a little straighter. "Okay, fair enough."

"Your other partners? Their history matters too."

"I don't have 'other partners', Sophie. I have you."

"What about Tiffany?"

"Jeezus, Sophie." He sat up and swung his legs over his side of the bed. He glanced back at her. "I've never had unprotected sex with anyone, and for your information no sex of any kind with Tiffany."

She didn't say anything. She didn't know what to say. His declaration confused her.

"Is that what you think of me? I'll fuck anyone, no matter the consequences? That I have no respect for my female partners, or myself?"

"I'm not going to apologize for asking." But because she could have been a tad more delicate she got up on her knees behind him. She risked wrapping her arms around his shoulders. "I don't think you're callous or uncaring. I'm a tad freaked out here. Okay? This isn't normal behavior for me. I don't know how to do whatever this is."

He shifted around to face her, put his hands in her hair. A small smile graced his lips and she breathed a little easier. "I guess both of us are going to have to stock up on condoms."

She dropped a kiss on his lips. "Thank you."

"In the meantime…" He rolled back taking her with him. Before she knew it she was trapped beneath him. His hands trapping hers over her head. "What did you do with my tie?"

She laughed. "I don't think so."

"I've heard rumors about this book everyone is reading…"

"Absolutely not."

"Not everyone's a fan then." He nibbled along her jaw.

"No need for knots." Her hands slipped free of his to frame his face. "I'm not going anywhere."

He kissed the ink decorating her shoulder. His fingers traced the lines down her back. "Tell me about this one."

"It was during my whimsical period." Her fingers twirled and caught in the strands of his hair.

He lifted his head. "Dandelions are whimsical?"

"The idea of seeds on the breeze of change?"

"Very…" His head dipped and his lips traced the path of the seeds blowing on the wind. "…you."

She swallowed back her words, explicit words, demanding words, as her hips shifted and her back arched. His fingers were there, stroking, rubbing, entering.

"Come for me," he whispered.

She obliged him.

Chapter Five

Sophie pushed through her front door, arms full of groceries, envisioning the hot steamy water of the bath, lots of bubbles and a glass of Caleb's wine. Kellie and the baby were at an appointment with Caleb. The house was empty leaving her with a few precious minutes of alone time. She figured the spa treatment would soak away sore muscles and give her a chance to indulge in the awkward anticipation of seeing Caleb.

She flicked on the lights and called out, "Marnie."

"I'm sorry to say she's not here."

She tracked his words on a puff of panic to a chair. Jason Drummond lounged indolent in her living room. His burly sidekick at attention behind him. She clamped a trembling hand over her mouth, trapping in the scream while juggling her produce. There was nothing she could do about the spike in heart rate except breathe and back the hell up.

"I need a moment of your time." He lifted a hand, signaled. "Why don't you help Dr. Monroe with her bags?"

Drummond swirled the contents of his wine glass and gave a delicate sniff. "Courtesy of Caleb I imagine. He has excellent taste." He shot a sneer around the room. "At least he used to, before he got tangled up with you."

"Don't like what you see, then get the hell out."

She held onto her bags instigating a childish game of tug of war. At the first tear she shoved the whole lot at him. Glee shot through her fear when he stumbled back.

"Bitch." He let it all drop and stepped toward her. Bags split open. Oranges, apples and cans of diet soda rolled around their feet.

Drummond sighed. "Enough."

She held up her middle finger and gave the big guy a flash of her pearly whites. His name calling was the very least of her worries. She faced the man in the chair. "On break from trolling high schools?"

Drummond's lip curled. "And here I thought you were too smart to believe a freak like your sister."

She pulled out her cell phone. "I'm calling the cops."

"I wouldn't if I were you." Jason nodded to his sidekick. He plucked her phone out of her hand. Drummond studied her while he swallowed back more of her wine. "About your sister..."

"What about her?"

"She came to see me last night."

Oh, Marnie, what have you done now?

His words a noose around the neck of any hope she had her sister might have the clarity of mind to do the sensible and right thing. Even for Kellie.

"I did warn her." He shrugged inside his two thousand dollar suit. "I'm no longer interested in being reasonable. It's unfortunate you've been caught up in this mess. But things being the way they are I'm forced to prove a point."

She remained silent. Not by choice. By sheer lack of saliva and courage. Reasonable? Nothing about him suggested he understood the concept.

"My reputation is on the line."

Moisture salted her tongue in a rush. The sheer egotism of his statement fueling a spark of unhelpful nastiness in her. "This would be your reputation as a serial cheater? Abuser? Snob? I'm confused."

"Because of the potential harm to my career and reputation I feel it only fair you and yours suffer your share of discomfort in return. Which brings me to some business between you and I."

"We don't have business together. I'm not telling you again. Get out. Caleb's on his way here. I don't think you want to be here when he arrives."

He tsked, reeking of snotty from his salon cut hair to his hand-stitched shoes. She wanted to slap his face. "Lying is such a nasty habit. I happen to know Caleb's escorting the little mother and her brat around town. It's amazing what a man will do to get some tail."

"Judging others by your own low standards?"

He snorted out a laugh. "You think Caleb has standards?"

Her chin went up.

"He's as guilty of thinking with his dick as the rest of us. Don't tell me he hasn't tried to get a taste of what's under those delightful hospital scrubs."

"Are you familiar with the term douchebag?" He was such a shit. "Silly me, of course you are. The veneer might spell GQ, but your center is a black hole. So, why don't we get to the reason you've violated my home."

Before Marnie walked through the door and things went from worse to horrible.

"By all means." His glass clinked against the little side table. Standing he was taller than Sophie remembered from the bar. His eyes never left her face as he tugged at the cuffs of his shirt. She refused to break eye contact. She fantasized about grabbing the side table lamp and smashing it up side his temporal lobe. He picked up a business-sized brown envelop from the table and handed it to her. "I did warn him. Like I warned your sister."

"Leave my sister alone." Sophie swallowed back the dread, took the envelope and opened it. The words blurred and she blinked back the disbelief. "A notice of eviction. I don't understand."

"I made the landlord of the building housing your clinic an offer he couldn't refuse. Once your lease is up I'm afraid you'll have to vacate the building."

"You can't do this." A hot flash of panic blindsided her. "This area needs this clinic."

"What the area needs is a proper clinic, run by a qualified doctor. One who's a little less experimental and a little more experienced. One who doesn't advocate for injection sites and shelters ignoring all the rules."

She could beg. Would beg for the sake of her patients. "You don't need to do this. I can talk to Marnie. She won't bother you again. Please."

"You're right. She won't."

She let out a grateful breath when the door opened. Jason motioned to the man at his side to move in the direction of the front door.

"What the hell is going on?" Caleb barged past Jason's lackey dragging a terrified Kellie behind him, fruit and pop cans scattering in every direction. He let go of her to turn Sophie around to face him. "Are you okay?"

"You insult me, Caleb. We were just conducting some business."

She caught a flash of fury before he rounded on the other man. "Business?"

Sophie handed Caleb the papers. "He brought this."

Caleb scanned the paper. "You go too far."

"And I thought we had a deal." Jason tipped a bored look in Kellie's direction. "Does she have to be here?"

"We do have a deal." Caleb put a hand on Kellie's arm. "And she stays because she's welcome here. Why don't you explain to me what you're talking about?"

In his first display of agitation, he jabbed at Caleb. "I thought I made it quite clear. I'm not a bank. People can't show up and expect to make withdrawals. Scream demands. Nobody speaks to me like that. No. One."

Baby Quinn followed up his father's words with a wail loud enough to alert the neighbors. Kellie tried to comfort him but he was having none of it.

"Get control of this situation, Caleb. I'm not telling you again."

He signaled his man and they strolled out. They left the door wide open. Through it they watched as a car rolled up in front of her place. The driver got out and opened the passenger side door. Jason Drummond climbed in without a backward glance. When they pulled away Sophie inhaled her first deep breath in what seemed like hours.

"Son of a bitch." Caleb's words were low and angry. His next ones not much better. He turned to Kellie. "Where is she?"

Kellie backed up at his tone. "I don't know. I swear."

Sophie closed her eyes. She scrubbed shaking hands over her face. "I haven't seen her since last night."

"Well, someone sure as hell better find her before she does worse damage. Kellie, where would she go if she were flush?"

"I don't know."

"Think."

Kellie flinched. "She'd head to Pigeon Park. From there she'd likely end up at the Balmoral. It's where I was staying."

Caleb headed for the door. Alarmed, Sophie trailed after him. "I'm coming with you."

"No. You're. Not." Three words, every one of them hard, succinct, and pissed off.

Okay. She understood he wanted to protect them. She did. But he had no idea about Pigeon Park or the Balmoral and what happened in those types of places. There was a code and he was getting ready to ram up against it. "You won't get anyone to talk to you."

He pulled out his money clip, flashed it and shoved it back in his pocket. "You're wrong."

"Caleb—"

"I'll be back."

He marched out the door before she could insist. She grabbed her cell phone from where Jason Drummond's goon had dropped it on his way out. Her text message was straight forward.

Think about it. U need my help.

He ignored it.

All she could see was Marnie grabbing the chef's knife or pointing her gun. Lows she'd never stooped to before. When caught off guard or cornered, she would defend her ground. The thought, coupled with the idea of Caleb wondering around a dark, secluded park asking questions from drug dealers scared her to death. She called for Kellie and grabbed her coat.

****

Caleb parked across the street from the Balmoral, one of the crumbling single room occupancy hotels providing low-income housing to tenants who could afford the meager rent. Despite the plunging temperature the street was busy. People came and went, pushing carts, clutching backpacks, stumbling, strolling and rushing. Early evening on a Friday night, the street was a wave of movement.

He reread her latest text. She was on her way. Unlike his response to her last ten missives, which had been silence, he took the time to reply.

In the lobby.

She was stubborn from the tip of her short haircut to her booted toes. He was in so much trouble where she was concerned. He spent too much time thinking about her. Craving her company. Picturing tomorrows. When he wasn't wondering around dark parks trying to avoid getting his ass kicked. Or worse.

Caleb climbed out of his nice warm vehicle and tugged up the collar of his coat. He glanced up at the building. Even with the dark hiding the worst of its problems it sagged. He'd struck out at the park, wasted valuable time on a wild goose chase. He was three hundred bucks poorer and tired as shit. It surprised him he still had energy left over for anger.

But he did.

He walked in and almost ran into a skinhead charging for the front door. He shoved past Caleb,

133

yanking up his hood and putting his face in the shadows of his coat. A watch worth more than six month's rent in this pit circled his wrist. Whatever. He pinched the area at the bridge of his nose.

The ugly swastika tattooed on the skin between his thumb and forefinger gave his tiredness permission to get the better of his tongue. "Watch it, asshole."

The guy didn't look back. Instead he offered up a backhanded middle finger salute before hitting the street.

"Nice," he muttered. It was a colossal mistake to come here. Control equaled rational. He was not in control. Of anything.

He was insane.

Evidenced by the fact he'd bribed a drug dealer.

Why?

Because he was churned up, turned on, and scared to death. Over falling in love? This level of insanity required nothing less than the L word. He shook his head too tired to be having this conversation with himself. Complicated relationship statuses were for later, or never, not the lobby of rancid hotels. Instead he made his way to the grimy front desk and bribed the greasy haired night manager for the room number.

Sophie rushed into the shabby lobby, spotted him, and stopped. Caleb shoved his hands in his pockets and resisted the urge to go to her. The worry was in her drawn face, in the dark circles framing her lovely eyes. It hunched her shoulders and kept her hands hidden. It rooted her to the spot. His anger evaporated. Disgust took its place. He was being an asshole.

She was an adult and this was her sister. She had every right to be involved. Truth was her knowledge of the area and its residents was an advantage he could have used. Even if it killed him to admit it.

He crossed the dirty floor. "218."

Wary, she nodded and headed for the elevator.

Caleb grabbed her arm. "Stairs. The guy at the desk says it's broken."

They took the stairs to the second floor. The only living being they encountered was a starved looking rat. Hellhole was too kind a word. On the second floor landing he breathed a sigh of relief, glad to be leaving the stench of the stairwell behind. Except the gagging combination of urine, cigarette smoke, and over nuked food followed them into the miserable hallway. Plaster crumbled off water-stained walls. Holes peppered the grimy plaster. Hope had died here and despair had rushed to fill the vacancy.

"God, how do people live like this?"

She flicked him a glance. "It's better than the street. Lack of affordable housing isn't a joke. We actually arranged for a city councilor to come and live in the DTES for two months with only the equivalent of a welfare check in his pocket. He stuck it out even though by the end of it he was reduced to binning."

"Binning?"

"Digging in the dumpsters for stuff to eat. Or sell. If they're lucky people leave the good stuff on top of the bin. That way the binners know there's a good chance it's hasn't spoiled yet."

Caleb stopped their progress down the hall. She looked up at him with tired green eyes. Resigned.

"I'm sorry." For once he had nothing else to say.

"For what? Being a clueless dick or for trying to shut me out of my own life."

Caleb blocked her way. Hadn't his mother always warned him to think twice and speak once? "You're right. I'm not up to speed on social justice issues. But I'm working on it. As for shutting you out? I don't want you here. To have you hear the things I need to make clear. So if that makes me a dick, then so be it."

She looked straight passed him.

Caleb sighed, gave up. "Come on, this way."

She didn't protest. He directed them down the hall. The door to 218 was ajar. Caleb knocked anyway. No one answered.

Sophie jostled her way past him. "Marnie."

Nothing. Caleb stepped into a tiny room crammed with stuff. It took a few seconds for him to identify the lump on the bed as human. A second more to realize something was very wrong.

"Oh, shit! Marnie." Sophie rushed to the bed, ordered him to call for help.

He yanked out his phone and dialed. On the bed Marnie was bleeding out of a hole in her chest. Her face was a bloody mess. He reached out to help and knocked over the almost empty bottle of vodka propped up beside her on the bed.

Sophie went to work. Caleb watched, too horrified, too focused on following her instructions to worry about all the blood.

But it was too late. Marnie lost consciousness. By the time the ambulance and the firefighters arrived she was unresponsive, her pulse nonexistent. Along with the unbelievable truth came the dizzying scents of sweat, blood, and death. Now Caleb stood in the squalid hallway, braced against the dirty wall, head spinning, fielding questions from police officers who'd responded to the call. They'd ordered him out of the room, needing the space. He provided as much information as he could while ambulance attendants worked with Sophie inside the room.

She refused to stop. Kept working to try and bring her sister back. In the end the attendants stepped back to let Caleb through. He stood behind her. He wrapped his arms around her and gently pulled her back and away from her sister's dead body. She sagged into him, lifted wild, disbelieving eyes to his.

He could only nod against the gravity sucking weight of her despair. It called forth his own when he wished to keep it hidden. He blinked back the sting of moisture. They both shuddered. He pressed her face into his chest to suffocate her words, her anguish. The frantic efforts of the last thirty minutes stopped. In a slow creep horror replaced panic and helplessness.

He tried to hoist her up scared they were both going to land in a heap on the soiled carpet. Her fists grasped at his jacket, clenching and unclenching. Her sobs scarred his soul. He shut his eyes but it didn't help. He was still there. His heart continued its ruthless beating, so hard his chest hurt.

He'd come looking for a fight. To threaten. Intimidate. To do whatever needed to be done to get her to stop screwing up. Now she was gone and there was nothing left to do but leave the professionals to the messy business of death.

He got them into the hallway without being aware of how he did it. His head was swimming, thoughts coagulating into clots of disbelief, anger, uselessness. Where were his coping skills? His inner Superman?

What he wouldn't give to leap a tall building, stop

a speeding train, instead of standing there doling out a measly amount of comfort like it was going to make any kind of difference. He ran a hand over Sophie's hair, held her up with the other. He coaxed, murmured meaningless platitudes as tears rained down her pale cheeks. Blood stained her hands, her clothes, there was a smear on her cheek. He was castrated by her grief.

"Sophie. Listen to me. We have to go home now."

Her look remained vacant. Then gripped by a thought she held up her hands and stared at them like she'd never seen them before.

"Here." After checking in and leaving her contact information with the police he searched out the communal bathroom and dragged her into it. When warm water ran from the taps he pushed her hands under the spray. Pink-red water filled the sink and swirled down the drain. He lifted his wet hand to her cheek and did the best he could with her face. His sweater did duty as a towel.

The distance to his car was the equivalent of a marathon. He tucked an unresponsive Sophie into the passenger side of his Range Rover. As he made his way to the other side of his vehicle he stripped off his soiled jacket and dumped it in an empty shopping cart pushed against a wall. He'd left the sweater he'd used as a towel on the bathroom floor. He shivered in the cold. If he could have done without his shoes and pants he'd have left those too.

He wanted to leave everything from the rat infested hotel behind, to take nothing of the misery back with him. He craved amnesia. To know he could walk away made it all worse. He hadn't asked for this. All he'd wanted was a date. With a woman who'd caught his eye. Lots of women had caught his eye. None of them had reached down and tried to rip out his soul on the second date.

The red and blue and yellow lights of various emergency vehicles flashed in the night behind him. His hand clenched around the driver's side door handle. They hadn't required anything but entertaining or jewelry. Maybe a sand and sex beach trip to St. Thomas. People rushed by him. They avoided the lights, the uniforms, intent on remaining invisible. He rested his forehead against the door, the ice cold window a balm for his shame. A tap on his shoulder made him jump. He jerked around.

A weathered old man huddled in a beat up old parka stretched his neck to get a closer look. "Hey, mister. You okay?"

Caleb closed his eyes and nodded. The guy didn't move. He sighed. "I'm good. Thanks."

He squinted at him. "You sure? You don't look too good."

"Rough night." Caleb scooped up a couple of dollar coins from his pant pocket.

The old man laughed, waved off the offer of money. "You take care now."

He indulged in a brief escape fantasy. Back to a reality he could handle. Then he set his self-pity aside and manned up. He drove her home. Inside she headed for the couch and perched at the end of it. Stunned confusion and sadness etched lines into her face.

He sat down on the coffee table across from her, their knees touching. She was a mess. The evidence of her valiant efforts ground into her clothes. Her eyes were red, the skin around them swollen and smudged with black. With gentle hands he undid her coat, slid it off her shoulders, dropped it to the floor. He pulled her boots from her feet. It all required incinerating.

He scanned the small space, listening. Nothing. Frowning, he asked, "Where's Kellie?"

"At a friend's. I dropped them off before…"

"Okay. Good. I'll be right back." First a garbage bag for her outer clothes. Next the bathroom. He bent over the tub and ran the water. He grabbed a bottle of body wash and squeezed. When the tub was filled with hot, soapy water he detoured to the kitchen and searched through her cupboards. Grabbing up a bottle of whiskey he poured a couple of fingers in a glass. He tipped the bottle up and chugged. Took a breather. And tipped the bottle up again.

Back in her front room he wrapped her fingers around a glass. "Drink."

She swallowed a sip and set it down on the table.

He offered his hand. "Come on. You need to get cleaned up."

She bit her lip, eyes glistening she looked up at him. "She's really gone this time."

"I know." Words deserted him as her tears tumbled over wet lashes. He bent down and gathered her up. "I've got you. Come on, let's get you cleaned up."

On the way past he snagged the bottle of whiskey. Her tiny bathroom smelled like warm gingerbread and the steam created a nice hazy screen. He found a space among her lotions and washes for the liquor bottle. "Do you want me to help? Or should I go? I won't be far, just outside the door."

A little focus came back to her eyes. She reached out for him. "Stay."

He ran a gentle hand down the side of her face. "Are you sure?"

Her head bobbed. "Pretty damn sure."

"Okay."

"Okay," she echoed.

"Let's get you out of these clothes." She struggled to get them off, but together they managed. Caleb grabbed a towel along with her dirty clothes. "Washing machine?"

Still in her underwear, she pointed across the hall to a closet. "Through there."

He shed his own clothes then stuffed everything in and guessed at a setting. He wrapped the towel around his hips. Back in the bathroom Sophie lay in the tub focused on the ceiling. He closed the toilet seat and sat down.

"Sorry, I had to wash mine too."

"You're going to freeze."

"I'll be fine."

"Caleb, while I appreciate the heroics, you need to wash off too. And if you're half as frozen as me, you need to warm up. So get in the damn tub."

"Bossy," he muttered. He lost the towel and she scooted forward. But he was grateful to have some of her back with him. Any of her.

"Marnie and I called a spade a spade. It was one thing we had in common."

He crawled in behind her, grabbed the bottle of whiskey and swilled back a mouthful. He could do this. Be the friend she needed. Provide comfort. Without dissolving into a mindless mess. Chest deep in bubbles he pulled her back and settled her against his heart. He handed her the bottle. After a healthy mouthful she gave it back.

"Hard to argue with the facts." He reached for a bottle of shampoo and squirted some onto the top of her head. "But there had to be more attractive qualities you shared."

He worked some suds into her hair. Rinsed. Repeated. He moved onto her stiff shoulders, satisfied when they rolled and stretched under his fingers.

"We both loved waffles."

"Waffles?" A little out of left field but it was a start.

"And The Breakfast Club."

"The Breakfast Club, huh? Lean forward."

She obliged. "You know? The movie?"

"Yeah, I got the reference. I was more of a Ferris Bueller fan myself." He picked up a spongy thing and squeezed on some bath gel, worked up a lather.

"Of course, you were."

"Although Molly Ringwald was pretty hot." He handed it to her to use. "What else?"

"Black nail polish." She raised a soapy foot out of the water.

"The Goth doctor."

"Has a certain ring." She sighed. Her head lolled against his shoulder. "Marnie would have appreciated it."

"I know." He didn't know what else to say. To hide the lack he washed his own hair. It took everything he had to raise his arms. By the time he'd gotten them both rinsed off and out of the tub he remembered his clothes were in the washing machine. He left her to dry off and put them in the dryer. He was standing in the hall in a towel when she emerged from the bathroom.

"How can I be so tired yet so damn awake?"

A spot of lotion clung to her cheek. He smoothed it out. "I wish I knew what to say to make this easier."

"I don't think there are any words." She laced her fingers through his. "You must be ready for sleep. You look exhausted."

"Pretty damn exhausted." He brushed his thumb over her knuckles. "I'll take the couch."

"Sounds lonely." Her lips twitched. She squeezed his hand. "Think you can handle holding me while I sleep."

"White knight, remember?" He tugged her closer, wrapped his arms around her. Small and desolate to his lank and weary, they were a sad set. Her arms came around him and he rested his chin on her damp hair. He pulled her scent deep into his lungs.

"Thank you." Her cheek was cool against his chest. He felt her sigh, the faint sweep of her lashes.

"No problem, my lady." Except it was a problem. White knight? More like the court jester. A joke. At least to Jason Drummond. They would see who had the last laugh. "Let's go."

He tucked her under the covers and crawled in beside her. They had simply shed towels, were too weary to worry about being naked. It didn't matter. Any erection he might have sported fizzled the moment he closed his eyes. His brain played a slideshow of blood, death, and squalor. No one should have to die, or live, in filth. The thought of Kellie spending months in that dirty hovel of a room cranked up his agitation. In the dark Sophie shifted and Caleb did the same.

The hours passed, filled with intermittent dozing and furtive glances at the bedside clock. Sophie tossed and turned beside him. At five o'clock in the morning he gave up and went to the kitchen to make coffee.

To map out his plan.

****

Sophie found him in the kitchen, brooding in the almost dark. A hint of morning on the horizon. The comforting scent of coffee drifted from the pot on the counter. He was dressed, her clothes from the night before neatly folded and stacked on the table. His pen posed silent over a notepad. She tightened the sash on her robe. He'd been up for a while. Tiredness was etched into grooves on his forehead, around his grim mouth.

Sophie hadn't liked waking up alone, panicky and reaching for him. He'd come to mean a lot in a very short period of time. And on the very worst morning of her life that knowledge pissed her off.

Possessed of some kind of freaky sixth sense he looked up. "Morning. Coffee's on."

"Thanks." She scooped up the stack of clothes, opened the lid on the trashcan and tossed them in. He watched her saying nothing. She braced her hands on her hips. "So, what are you working on?"

"Just some thoughts on Kellie's case."

She poured coffee into an extra-large mug. The hot, dark liquid did little to soothe her. She went to stand next to him. He didn't reach out, or try to touch her. She felt the loss of comfort all the way down to her toes.

"The sooner we get things worked out the better." He bent his head and flipped the notebook closed, hiding whatever it was he'd written. He lifted his head. "How are you feeling?"

She shrugged. "Crappy, thanks for asking."

"I'm sorry. I wish I could make it better." His oh-so-careful tone matched his anemic smile.

Okay. He didn't know what to do with her this morning. How to pat her hand. She got it. But she had more pressing things to worry about then Caleb's sensibilities. "Hard to make murder okay."

"I know."

She wanted to punch something. "Drummond's behind this. I know he is."

He rubbed his forehead. "I'm sure the police will figure it out."

She snorted. "That's make one of us."

He set his pen down. Placed it precisely parallel to his notepad. He straightened it in a snobby kind of double check. "You need to leave Jason to me."

"Excuse me?"

He sighed. "How about we deal with today. And getting through it."

His tone, his dismissal, scrapped against the jagged edge of her very last nerve. Her bitchiness rose with every flick of his eyelashes. "That's it? How many times are we going to have this discussion? This is my life. You can't shut me out of it."

"I'm not shutting you out of anything. I'm trying to help."

He wore reasonable like a suit. Too bad she wasn't falling for the act. She didn't have to. She wasn't one of his clients. "I didn't ask for an intervention."

"Most don't." His tone was dry as dirt.

"I want you to listen to me. To hear me."

"All right. You're right." His jaw tightened. "It's still a big accusation."

For some much needed warmth she clasped her hands around her mug. "He had the most to gain."

"Okay." Her man of many words kept it short.

"Don't pat me on the head determined to be stoic and supportive because it's what poor Sophie needs."

He shifted in his chair, his expression cool. "What do you want me to say? You want me to say I think Jason is capable of murder? He's a lot of things, but a murderer?"

"I want you to admit it's a possibility. Acknowledge I'm not being a paranoid wreck."

"You're under a lot of stress."

"So, I am being a paranoid wreck."

"I didn't say that." He pushed back from the table. On his feet he put the short length of the table between them. "Look, I need to get going. I need to stop by my condo. It's Saturday but I need to go into work for a couple of hours. I'll be by later. We'll talk then and we'll come up with a plan."

"A plan?"

"Yes, a plan." He stood and gathered up his phone, tore a couple of pages free of the notebook. He set it aside. Much like he was doing with their relationship. Unless he didn't see it as a relationship.

"Things getting a little too messy for you, Caleb? It's time to un-complicate things? Get back to your world. Forget about the ugliness of all this." She set her coffee mug down on the table, swept a hand around the room.

"I think we're both too tired to talk right now. I have to get to work."

"No. I think we should talk about it right now."

"Sophie…"

"You're out of your comfort zone. But you can't push aside what happened. We need to talk about it."

"Easy to say." He shook his head. "Not so damn easy to do."

"So try a little harder."

"And why can't you understand I don't want to do this with you? I'm trying to make things better not worse." His pushed a hand through his hair. "So stop poking at me in an effort to avoid your own feelings. You're the one who needs to talk about last night, not me."

"I tried, you don't believe me." There wasn't a whole lot of room in her tiny kitchen but she managed to back up a step. To retreat. And there were those stupid tears again. She swiped at them, furious for doing this in front of him. Her heart was breaking and she was unraveling, leaving the threads of her confidence in a heap at her feet.

"Sophie—"

"Don't." She put out a hand to stave him off.

But he gathered her up. She wanted to resist the warmth, his comfort, but she didn't want to be alone in this swamp of sadness. His shirt was soft against her cheek, his chest solid. She sniffed and got a whiff of her soap and fabric softener. Giving in and holding on seemed like good medicine.

"I'm sorry. Please, don't cry." He ran a gentle hand over her sleep spiked hair. "We need to think this through, to be careful. We can't accuse him without evidence."

"I know." She sniffed. "I do. But I'm terrified no one will care about a dead junkie."

His arms tightened around her. "We care."

"I said I'd talk to her." She let go enough to point in the direction of the living room. "He stood right there, very confident Marnie would no longer be a problem."

His hands slid down her arms until they gripped her elbows. "It's not proof."

"I know."

He rubbed her arms, his eyes serious. "I need a couple of hours, but I'll be back."

She nodded.

"I promise."

"Go." She thought of her sister, the arrangements she needed to make, Kellie. The weight of those things bowed her shoulders. But they were private thoughts and she wanted to keep them close awhile longer. "I'll be fine."

He kissed her forehead, then raised her chin. Meeting his eyes was the hard part. "She loved you."

Sophie had never heard her say it. And now it was too late. Her sister was gone. Her worst nightmare had come to pass. Marnie was dead. Sophie had failed. In so many ways.

Love?

She hungered for it.

Marnie.

Liam.

She broke contact.

How many times did you chase the impossible?

Chapter Six

Caleb returned to his office with another refill of stale, office coffee. A couple of hours had stretched into four, six, then eight. Caleb scrubbed at the back of his neck. Knowing what needed doing and getting it done had taken some maneuvering. The sun was going down on a day spent ensuring the safety of the ones he loved.

With her scent covering him and images of their bath fresh in his mind, he birthed the impossible thought he might be in love with Sophie. He gulped another mouthful of lukewarm coffee. For the first time growing old with someone didn't smack of marriage roulette.

He wished he wasn't going to have to tell her Jason Drummond was going to get away with murdering her sister. There was no hard evidence to prove otherwise. None. Of course, the investigation was ongoing. The fine members of the Vancouver Police Department didn't like junkies turning up dead in filthy hotel rooms despite what Sophie assumed. They probably cared more than most. Caring didn't create leads or conjure up evidence.

A lot of blood. A lot of filth. A lot of people in and out. Small space. And rats. The only CSI capable of finding information of value played one on TV.

It didn't mean Jason Drummond wasn't going to pay. There was the matter of Sophie's clinic, Kellie's child support, and mayoral candidacies to address. He wasn't going to let any of those things go. And Caleb had a plan. Jason had been very careful in orchestrating his depravities while avoiding any hint of scandal. With one exception.

He hadn't spoken to Kimberley McKay in too many years. Not since she'd come to him for help and he'd brushed her off. Knowing the right questions to ask would be key. Nothing intrusive or insensitive. Often times the less you pushed the more you ended up learning. He'd forgotten everything he'd learned when he'd confronted Marnie. He'd pushed. Hard. He'd let anger overrule his good sense. Fear for Sophie had goaded him into making mistakes. Now her sister was lying on a slab in a morgue.

He paced to the bank of windows rimming his corner office phone in hand, Kimberley's number written on a slip of paper. No, he couldn't prove Jason Drummond was a murderer. His fingers tightened around the piece of paper, crushed it into a ball. But he'd still pay, and with more than money. Caleb was going to hit him were it hurt. There would be no legacy. No votes for or against. No public office. No limelight.

"Caleb."

He turned at the sound of his name and the accompanying knock. Devin Donnelly, fellow lawyer and friend, walked into Caleb's office with a sheaf of papers in his hand and a jangle of keys. He set the lot down on Caleb desk.

"Thanks," offered Caleb.

Devin nodded an acknowledgment. "When you're ready we can go over everything. Dot our i's and cross our t's. Then I can meet Kellie next week and we'll go from there."

"Great. I appreciate it."

Devin hesitated, hands shoved in the pocket of his pants. "You're sure about this?"

Caleb nodded in his direction, smiled even though he dug deep to find it. "Kellie will make an excellent condo sitter while you're in Dubai. I'll keep tabs on her."

Devin didn't look convinced. "I know I don't have the whole story." He held up a hand. "And I don't need to know it. Just take care of yourself, man."

"Never doubt it."

"Okay then." Devin saluted as he headed out the door. "You know where I am if you need me."

Caleb made another call first. Secured a lunch date for Monday, New Year's Eve. His heart hurt with the weight of what he had planned. It didn't stop him. He punched in Kimberley's number. Getting away with murder was going to come with a very high price tag. But being someone's judge, jury, and executioner wasn't going to come cheap either. There was no way to avoid moral bankruptcy when you were deciding who to sacrifice as collateral damage.

****

Sophie opened the door at Caleb's knock. The rush of cold air cooled her cheeks, relief dampened the burn of grief. She needed him and there he stood on her stoop with a tray of to-go cups in his hand.

"A round of hot chocolate." He lifted the tray and even though a smile whispered at the corners of his mouth his eyes told the real story. Tired with dark circles underneath, but still warm, compassionate, caring.

"How's it going?" he asked.

Sophie stepped aside to let him in. "Not as bad as I'd expected, but still…bad."

"How's Kellie?" Caleb handed her the cups and shrugged out of his coat, hung it on a hook.

"Devastated." She put a hand on his arm when he stepped in the direction of her front room. "And confused. I don't know how much more she can take without breaking."

He moved in closer. Sophie noted his regret in the soft knuckles he brushed across her cheek. "Understandable. But I need to talk to her. I have questions. I need answers."

"Maybe now's not the best time to press her. She's in a very fragile state."

"I'll take care with her. If Jason is going to pay for what's he done, I need those answers."

When they turned, Kellie was there. There was only one word to describe her: destroyed.

"She wouldn't leave me." Kellie looked to Caleb, tears in her voice. "She wouldn't. Not without a fight."

Sophie handed the cups back to Caleb and gathered her into her arms, murmured comforting platitudes even though it was her loss too. She led her into the living room, sat down beside her on the couch, pulled the young girl into her arms and pressed her head to her shoulder.

Caleb sat down on the coffee table directly in front of Kellie and put a hand on her knee. The scent of chocolate drifted around them but no one reached for the cups he'd set down beside him. "I know this is hard. You loved her. Relied on her."

The fear was in the jerk of Kellie's body. She

turned closer into Sophie.

Caleb continued, "I also know Marnie wanted you to have the means and the opportunity to look after Quinn. I can make her wishes a reality. If he's going to pay for what he's done I need the whole story. If there's anything you're holding back you need to tell us. Before it's too late."

Sophie pulled a blanket off the back of the couch and wrapped it around Kellie. "She wanted you safe. More than anything. No matter what. Nothing you say can hurt her anymore."

More tears threatened. Caleb handed Kellie a tissue and she sniffed into it. "None of it matters if she's gone."

"Not true," Sophie said. She hugged her close. "It matters more. She'd want you to do whatever it took. To be a survivor."

Caleb took over. "I know this is hard but I need you to tell me the absolute truth of what happened with Jason. Marnie's part in the blackmail scheme, as hard as it might be to tell it. Yours, as well."

"What does it matter now? Besides, you already know the story."

"But maybe not all of it." Sophie added an extra squeeze of comfort to her words.

"The truth always matters. If your speculations are right, maybe you'll remember something important. A small detail can make all the difference."

It was there, in the slump of her shoulders, the promise of more dead weight confessions. Sophie braced for more heartbreak.

"Marnie had debts." Kellie shot a guilty look at Sophie then Caleb. "Big ones."

"How much money did Marnie owe?" asked Caleb.

Kellie hung her head. "Forty thousand dollars."

Sophie closed her eyes and gathered Kellie in closer. "How…"

"She was bad into it with the drugs, then she lost something she was transporting. Something way valuable. She wouldn't tell me what it was." She snuggled in deeper. "Only that she had no choice to borrow from Poacher to make it right."

"Wonderful." Sophie massaged her forehead. An old threat from a sideways direction. She should have known, should have remembered. Caleb frowned at her wanting answers. She wet her lips, swallowed. "He's an old school loan shark with ties to Hell's Riot."

Caleb frown deepened. "So this Poacher person, you think he may have killed her?"

"Being dead makes it a little hard to collect your money. He likes knives. He has a signature. Marnie knew that better than anybody." Kellie shivered in her arms. Sophie drew a deep breath in, let it out. Marnie was out of everyone's reach now. "Hell's Riot owns the poverty industry down here. Poacher is one of the last of the old-school-style loan sharks left. Nowadays it's payday loan centers, pawn shops, rent-to-own. But if you have no paycheck, nothing to pawn…"

Kellie stepped in. "And you need big money…"

Sophie finished it. "You go to Poacher."

Sophie didn't think it had sunk in yet but it would. And she was right. It didn't take long.

"Jesus, her scar. She borrowed money from him before." At Sophie's nod, he ran a hand over his mouth, held it there. He was taking a moment, rearranging ideas in his head. A couple of seconds later, he said,

"One thing at a time. I want you to tell me how this all ties in to Jason. Your time with him."

Kellie closed her eyes. "He was supposed to be an easy mark. It was all supposed to be easy."

"Start at the beginning and go from there," Caleb prompted.

"Marnie knew his preferences."

"Marnie? She was the one supplying the girls?" Caleb's hands clenched into fists. He dropped them to his thighs, pressed down. His whole body tensed. Mouth shut tight, he traced his top teeth with his tongue. Fury hardened the lines of his face, his skin stretching to contain it.

"Caleb. Don't." Not here. Not now. She needed him to save that anger for later. For her.

He pulled it all back in. "Which were?"

In her arms Kellie cringed. Sophie shot him a pleading look. The one he gave back was unapologetic. She shook her head at him.

He ignored her. "It's important. Kellie?"

Sophie's hand found Kellie's and she held on, gave it a squeeze of support.

"She knew the drill and she'd arranged it all before. Loads of times. Jason trusted her to keep to their deal. And even though he likes his kink he's a safer bet than a lot of johns out there. I knew she needed money so I begged her to let me do it."

"Do what? Exactly."

"Set up Jason Drummond." She sat up a little straighter and sighed. "She refused at first but things got really bad with Poacher and she needed his fee so she caved. It gave her enough to tide Poacher over for a couple of months. So, I did myself up how he liked and it started."

A muscle jumped along Caleb's jawline. Sophie's heart pounded and like so many times in the past few days she knew she didn't want to hear what was coming next.

"Tell me." Not gentle, not threatening. But you knew he was serious. He wanted answers. He picked up a cup handed it to her. "Here, have a drink. Take a moment."

Kellie wrapped her hands around the warm cup and sipped. It took more than a moment but she finally looked up. Her voice was small, scared, and worst of all, ashamed. "I'm small and blond so I didn't have to dye my hair, just put it up in pigtails. No makeup, only clear lip gloss. Marnie arranged for the uniform."

"Uniform?"

It came out in a rush, like she wanted the telling over and done with as quickly as possible. "School girl. You know, short plaid skirt, white shirt, buttons down the front, vest to match the skirt, knee high white socks, Converse sneakers. White cotton panties. Nothing else. No exceptions."

Sophie clamped down on the bile fighting its way up her throat. Disgust showed on Caleb's face before he could mask it, but no surprise he didn't ask her to elaborate and Sophie was grateful.

"The blackmail?"

"We had a plan."

"Get pregnant and collect child support? Seems extreme."

"Caleb," Sophie warned.

Kellie ignored her. "No. The pregnancy was an accident. Honest. It was supposed to be the same arrangement as with the other girls. Get paid to have play dates then disappear. But Marnie planned to outsmart him and get extra. And he liked me. I was a favorite of his."

"So, you planned on getting more than the original twenty thousand plus what Marnie knew she'd get for arranging the meetings?"

Kellie nodded.

"Which all went to Marnie?"

"Yes. It had to. She needed it." Kellie pushed her hair back.

"And when you learned you were pregnant?"

"Marnie wanted me to have an abortion and we kind of figured it was the opportunity we needed to ask for some more cash."

"So you went to Jason?"

She nodded. "Another ten thousand on the condition he never saw me again. He made it pretty clear that meant ever."

"We know you didn't go through with it."

"I couldn't."

"The money?"

"Went to Marnie."

"What happened next?"

"Marnie was upset I didn't follow through with the abortion. Babies cost money. She said he was going to have to own up and be a father. She figured Jason would pay to keep everything quiet but we couldn't tap him for more until things settled a bit. Then we'd get our last twenty thousand. Ten for Marnie, ten for me."

"And then?"

She rubbed her arms. "Nothing happened until Jason saw me at the fundraiser about two months ago."

"How did you hear about the job for the fundraiser again?"

"Marnie arranged it for me. I was trying to work all the hours I could wherever I could."

"Jason says Marnie came to him after the fundraiser asking for more money."

"If she did she didn't tell me."

"How did Marnie break her arm?" Caleb asked.

"She fell down some stairs one night. It was dark. She tripped." But she avoided eye contact, choosing instead to pick up her cup and sip more not chocolate.

"Was it before or after the fundraiser?"

She hesitated, then shrugged and answered, "I'm pretty sure it was before."

"Here's what I think. I think Marnie did go to Jason and he got angry, refused to pay her. Instead he came after you. Threatened you."

"That's why Marnie made us hide." Tears threatened. "Until the baby was born. See, I'm telling you he killed her."

"There's no proof. No evidence to suggest Jason killed Marnie."

"Marnie went to see him on Friday night asking for the last twenty thousand." It came out on a whisper. "She said it was only fair. She said he deserved to pay. For everything. She was supposed to collect the money last night. Now she's dead." She twisted out of Sophie's arms and sat forward facing Caleb. "What if he comes after me?"

Caleb took her hand, held it between his own. "Marnie was a wild card. There was no way to control her. To trust she wouldn't keep popping up whenever she needed money. You're easier to manipulate and you have your son to protect."

"I want to be a good mother to Quinn. I want to support us, but I don't see how I can."

"By keeping things simple. And legal. If he's the father he's obligated by the courts to pay child support. Even if he voluntarily relinquishes his parental rights. I have a friend. He's leaving for a year in Dubai. He's looking for someone to condo sit. You can live there for a year rent free. Get yourself together, start a new life."

When had he managed to arrange it? Sophie sat back dumbfounded. Things were happening too fast. It was too crazy.

Kellie shook her head. "And if he decides he doesn't want to pay child support? We're an embarrassment to him. What's to stop him from coming after us?"

"I'm going to stop him."

Sophie locked gazes with him. The determination she saw there scared the hell out of her.

He looked to Kellie. "Marnie didn't use anything else to blackmail Jason, no pictures, no videos?"

He'd thought of everything.

"I don't think so. It was part of Marnie's fee. Making sure the girls didn't leave with any evidence. It was her job to make sure they never contacted him again. And they never did. That's why Jason kept coming to her. Marnie kept her word. Always."

"Except for this time."

"She was in a real bad place."

"And that's an excuse for blackmail?"

"No. But I know there weren't going to be any more girls after me."

"Why?"

"She said she was done. After she fixed things with Poacher. She didn't give a reason." Head down she continued in a low voice. "But...I think she was going to try and get clean. Debts cleared, fresh start, that kind of thing. She was going to do it for me. And for Quinn. Because I have to tell you, I don't think Jason broke her arm. I think Poacher did. She was super scared and it wasn't of Drummond."

Sophie closed her eyes. She knew her sister. Marnie would think she could contain someone like Drummond. Her turf. Her terms. The advantage. "So she took on the lesser of two evils."

Chapter Seven

Sophie hid out in the kitchen on the pretense of tidying up for the evening. Once again tears threatened. She tossed her damp tea towel down on the countertop.

She would not cry. Would. Not. Her butt hit the hard seat of a kitchen chair, her elbows braced on her thighs, head in her hands. She counted to ten. Then twenty. The pressure eased. One hundred.

Strong hands squeezed her shoulders. It startled her enough to have her lifting out of her chair.

"No. Sit." His thumbs dug into her shoulder blades. A guilty sigh of pleasure escaped. Her shoulders tensed up.

"Breathe." Down her back and up again. The base of her skull. Shoulders again.

"So good." Her muscles unraveled under his manipulations. She let her head fall back. He came around to kneel in front of her. "Better."

She nodded.

Concern darkened his eyes. He trailed a finger down her cheek. "It's been a long day."

"For you too." She tried to smile. And failed. "You've been busy making your own kind of arrangements, figuring things out. Making it all better."

He pulled another chair over. Sat down. Took her hands in his. "Back in there? Earlier? It was hard to hear. I'm sorry."

"It's not your fault. It all needed to be said." She gave his hand a squeeze. "I'm sorry too. I meant to tell you about Marnie providing the girls, but things spiraled so quickly I didn't get to it." She shook her head wanting, needing to be honest. "That's not the truth either. I just didn't want to have that conversation. Liam hated having to deal with Marnie and the havoc she created. I think part of me worried I'd be handing you the reason to walk away. "

"Hey." He brought one of her hands to his lips, brushed a kiss against her knuckles. "I don't scare that easy. Besides I was raised on drama. Not your kind of family issues, but Quinn family relations don't always run smooth."

She was willing to bet there wasn't a pimp in their ranks. "You're not a mirage or anything, are you? I mean you're real, right? Flesh and blood real? Not something my traumatized mind has made up to deal with all the crazy, mind warping stuff that's happening?"

A small smile tipped the corners of his mouth. "Here I thought I made more of an impression the other night."

She tipped her head, searched his face, lifted a hand to his cheek. "I don't think I could do this without you."

"I'm not going anywhere." He wrapped a hand around hers, held it in place. "Are you up for talking about this some more?"

No.

"Yes."

He got up put the kettle on, arranged their chairs closer to the table. When it was set with cups and the steeping tea pot he sat back down. "I called one of my buddies with the Vancouver Police Department. He works in the Major Crime Division."

Busy indeed. "Did they find out anything?"

"Homicide is looking into her death. But so far their investigation hasn't turned up anything significant."

She read between the lines. "And they aren't going to spend valuable man hours trying to find the murderer of a junkie."

"Not true. They're doing everything they can, but no one's talking. No one saw anything. No one knows anything."

Needing something to do, Sophie reached out and poured their tea. Everything was such a mess. Regret stacked her *what ifs* into one teetering tower. She pushed to her feet as they tumbled out of her mouth. "If she'd only come to me. Asked me for the money. Trusted me enough for the truth."

Caleb followed her. "It's not your fault."

"But I was getting through to her." Her voice wobbled. She cringed. "You heard Kellie, she was going to quit."

He stepped in front of her, his hands capturing her cheeks. "It wasn't Marnie's fault either. The person who murdered her is the one responsible for her death."

"We're never going to know for sure, are we?"

The truth was in his shadowed eyes.

"If I could change things, I would. For you, I would."

She closed her eyes, pressed her forehead into his chest. "They aren't coming."

His arms tightened around her. "Who's not

coming?"

"My parents. For the funeral." She cleared her clogged throat. "My mother insists my father isn't well enough to make the journey. They're going to hold their own memorial later, in the summer, for the rest of the family."

"Sophie."

"No. It's fine." But the tears came despite her resistance, his comfort. She swiped them away. "Marnie hasn't existed for them for a long time. They're elderly. This will be easier for them."

"But not for you."

Trust Caleb to get it. She didn't want to bury her sister on her own. Didn't want the sole responsibility of laying her to rest.

"I'm here," he said.

She let out a laugh. She pushed back what she resolved were the last tears of the day. Rolled her eyes, looked up into his. "Lucky you."

His lips stopped a hair's breath away from hers. His hands slipped through the strands of her hair. "Exactly."

His lips were so warm against hers. In the dark, behind closed eyelids, she felt the swipe of his tongue. More warmth. No. Heat. And she wanted to absorb it all.

Her mouth opened and she let him in, free to do what he wanted as long as he didn't stop. It calmed the crazy in her head, leaving her feeling less lost and helpless. Less hopeless. He pulled her in closer, his hand on her waist, one on her cheek. Not pressing. Not leading.

Her hands fumbled over the wrinkled linen of his

dress shirt, over the unbuttoned section at his neck. Down sleeves rolled up to his elbows, across his broad back. The scrape of stubble on his neck and along his jawline was rough under her mouth. The stiff strands of hair at the base of his skull tickled her fingertips. It turned soft and tempting as she moved upwards and grabbed hold and captured his mouth.

He had big hands. Better to hold the world up with. They cradled her head and she sighed. He was preparing to stop the kiss. It was in the little nips, his own sigh. When he lifted his head her eyelids were slow to drift open, weighted down by passion and exhaustion. She didn't want to let the moment go.

"I needed that."

"Yeah?" She tried for a smile, to show some thankfulness. "Me too."

"Something else is wrong?"

"I'm worried about Kellie. She's so silent. So still. I know she talked earlier, but that was different. She's shutting down, just when she was starting to open up. He's taken one more thing from her. From someone who can't afford the loss. It makes me sick. How's he managed to hide it all for so long? Those goons who trail along behind him? He must pay them a lot to keep quiet."

"I don't think he picks them for their IQ level. Having said that, they're smart enough to know to keep their mouths shut."

"I'd say you were right, judging by the two he had with him at the Empress."

"I could try and talk to them. Get them to tell me something."

"No. Promise me." She grabbed fistfuls of his shirt.

"They're bad news. I got as close as I could to them that night at the bar. The hairy one is dumber than a bag of hammers. The skinhead was a whole different story. He made my skin crawl."

He tipped his head. "Wait a minute. Skinhead as in bald?"

"Definitely bald, but he also had this mean swastika tattooed on his hand." She shuttered. "You know, between his thumb and forefinger."

"A swastika?" He looked past her, his eyes not resting but shifting.

She reached out and smoothed the lines gathered across his brow. "I know, right?"

"And you saw him at the Empress?" he persisted.

"Yes." She frowned at him. "Am I missing something here?"

He turned away. She grabbed his arm and pulled him back. "No. No holding back."

"In the lobby. At the Balmoral. I was walking in when this guy ran into me on his way out. Bald. 5'11." The faraway look was back in his eyes. He grimaced. "I remember his watch. Expensive. Very. But he also had a swastika tattooed right here. On his way out the door he pulled up the hood of his coat, gave me the finger. I saw it. I saw him."

Sophie looked to where he pointed between his thumb and finger. "Oh my God."

He snapped his fingers. "That's it. That's the connection."

"Between Drummond and Marnie's murder." It wasn't much but it was something. And something was exactly what she needed right now.

"It's not proof." He smoothed a strand of hair

behind her ear. His touch as cautious as his words. "Of anything."

"It's proof enough for me." And it was. It was confirmation that self-righteous bastard had murdered her sister.

His hands went from cupping her face to gripping it. "You are not law enforcement."

"It's something." She pushed against his chest.

He didn't budge. "We'll go to the police with what we know. They'll take it from there."

"My faith in urban policing is a little low to say the least."

"Doesn't matter. It's for them to investigate." He relaxed his grip, his thumbs stroking, but the warning was still there. "We'll concentrate on the child support issue."

"Marnie got in his way and she's dead. Forgive me if I don't trust him to honor the law and pay the expenses of a child he refuses to acknowledge." She tried to push back. He refused to let go. She wanted him to understand. To agree with her. To fight with her. "What happens next year or when Quinn's old enough to ask about his father? When he's old enough to go looking for him on his own?"

A muscle jerked along his jawline. "By then it will be old news. He'll have thought of a way to spin it and come out looking pretty."

His mask was slipping, his well-meaning softness fading. Her need for reassurance shifted into a need to strike a blow of her own. "Is that how rich people do it? You don't believe Jason Drummond is going to let this go any more than I do. He's going to find a way to get rid of them. We won't know when. Or where. Or how.

We won't be able to stop him."

"You continue to underestimate me." His mouth flat lined, his cheekbones harsh points under cold eyes.

It was her turn to feel the burn of panic. She grabbed onto his arms to hold him in place. "What are you planning? So help me, Caleb, if you're plotting something you need to tell me."

He stiffened under her hands. "I won't let him hurt Kellie or Quinn or you."

"You can't spend the rest of your life being the vigilante to his villain."

"I'm capable of doing whatever it takes."

She gave him a shove. "Why are the good guys always so clueless? Don't you get it? There are different rules down here. You can't just will it and make it so."

He stepped back. "True. It's not like I'm the dedicated doctor giving her life to helping the less fortunate."

"Caleb."

"But I can spend it being the careless rich guy." He put a couple more feet of space between them. "Stick with what I know."

"That's not what I meant."

He turned back. "Right."

"It's not." She wouldn't love him if it were true. If he were the man he described. He was so much more. She put a hand to her stomach. Gave herself a second to regroup. To acknowledge the truth. "I don't want to spend the next decade wondering what he's going to do."

"I can handle Jason. He won't be allowed to hurt Kellie or his son. Be mayor. Or get rich off gentrification schemes."

"Wait. What schemes?"

He rubbed a hand over his forehead. "One thing at a time."

"Again, since I didn't get a satisfactory answer, what are you planning?" Her stomach lurched. By making himself a target? "I want to know. I deserve to know and you need to trust me enough to tell me."

"I'm going to a party."

She blinked. "Excuse me?"

"It's going to be next to impossible to prove Jason arranged for Marnie's murder. The only thing we have is a connection between Jason and Marnie and a connection between Jason is this skinhead."

"So what do we do?"

"I'm going to attend the Drummond's annual New Year's Eve party. I'm invited, although I'm pretty sure he's not expecting me to show up."

"And how's this going to help us?"

"I'm going to start by having a little chat with Jason and making it clear he won't be announcing his intentions to run for mayor."

"And what am I going to be doing during all this? Looking pretty?"

"You'll be here where I don't have to worry about you."

For real? "I do not think so."

"Sophie, this will be easier if I know you're safe. If I know Kellie and Quinn are too."

Then they heard it. Weeping coming from the living room. The sound of crying was quick to disappear, stifled. Caleb dropped his head to stare at the floor. He lifted it on a deep breath in then out. She shook her head at his silent question. "I'll go. It'll be easier for her."

He nodded. "I'll be here if you need me."

****

She crept out of Kellie's room, Quinn's soft breathing keeping time with his mother's. She indulged in one last glance back. Safe and sound. But for how long?

Out in the hall she paused in the soft glow of the muted nightlight. No sound of Caleb or the television. She checked and his coat was hanging in her small front vestibule. He'd left his keys, some loose change, and his phone on the kitchen table. An empty glass sat beside a bottle of whiskey, the ice cubes melting into water.

That left her bedroom.

She found him in bed taking up more than his share of the space and blankets. Fast asleep with an arm flung over his head, he didn't move an inch. His clothes and a towel in a heap beside the bed. She shed her clothes. Not an eyelid flickered. Like him she left her clothes where they fell.

She settled on the mattress, and he shifted in his sleep, turning onto his side to face her. His breathing remained deep and even. She waited before edging under what covers she could pull free. Her eyes drifted shut. Images flashed, old and new memories. She tried a new position, counting back from a thousand. She got to 976 when he reached over and tugged her closer. Her back to his chest.

"Go to sleep."

"I'm trying. It's not working." But she settled into him, his warmth to tempting to resist.

His hand settled over the no-man's land under her breasts, not brushing up against anything obvious and making no move to venture lower. "My favorite place in the world is this spot on St. Thomas. A private beach where the sun always shines and the water's always warm. It's my happy place."

"I'm sure it has more to do with your companion of the moment."

His smile brushed against her ear. "I'm not going to lie, usually the sex is pretty damn great."

She elbowed him in the stomach. It was her turn to smile when he huffed out a shot of air. "Brag much?"

His arms tightened around her. "Maybe I'm fishing for compliments. Anyway, it's where I go after a difficult negotiation, vicious court battles. Or after I'm forced to spend prolonged amounts of time in the presence of both my parents. Mental detox."

"Bad, huh?"

"The job is the job. It's what I signed up for and I'm not sorry I did. But it's different with my parents. It's personal. It's been fifteen years and they haven't moved on, not even enough to find someone else."

"I'm sorry."

"Don't be. They're adults acting like children. My point is, in the coming days you're going to need a happy place."

She was beginning to think it was right here in her bed with him. "I don't know if I have one. I've been so focused these last years, whether it was on becoming a doctor or lately as an activist, nothing else mattered."

Which put her relationship with Liam in bright, blinding perspective.

"Those photographs on the wall in your living

room tell a different story."

Surprised, she craned her neck back to look at him. "What do you mean?"

"Just because those scenes aren't bathed in sunshine, or aren't glossy or pretty? Doesn't mean they aren't beautiful. Or that the people you fight for can't be your happy place. They're your strength. When you're overcome with the arrangements of burying your sister, when you're feeling guilty over not being able to save her, take a walk on the streets you both loved and remember what it is to do good."

Her heart stilled its hammering at his last words. He knew what was going through her head, the worry there, and wasn't afraid to say it straight out. It took a little of the tiredness away. She shifted around so she was right flush against him. You couldn't have slipped a piece of paper between them.

"You're very good with words."

He brushed a hand over her hair, tugging at the short ends hugging her neck before moving on to stroke her cheek. "I think it's pretty evident once I stop talking things are going to get awkward."

She bit her lip and tried to keep the smile out of voice. "That's quite the invitation you've got going on down there."

"Sorry." He groaned and rolled away from her. He grabbed onto his hair like he was grabbing for his sanity. "You're tired and I'm tired. I'm trying to be a gentleman. But it's not working. You're too naked. And you smell too good. And taste too good…"

He tossed the covers back and moved to sit up. It didn't take much to stop him. A one handed gentle push to the chest and he was flat on his back again. She slid one leg over his thighs, careful to go real slow. "I think you smell pretty good too. And you're all nice and warm."

His eyes tracked her movements, his jaw muscle jumping as she settled into place. Once she stilled he held her hips in place. "Are you sure this is a good idea?"

She nodded. "Very, very sure."

"Just checking." His fingers squeezed her flesh. The gritty tone of his voice was a balm to her hurt. "I'm on board as you can probably tell."

"I miss my sister. But as complicated as our relationship was, she led me to my calling." She ran a finger down his chest, through the hair covering his belly button and lower. She skimmed the tip of his erection. "Know what she'd say right now?"

His weight shifted under her and his hands grasped at the covers. "Not without deflating the mood, so to speak."

She laughed and it felt so good. "She'd say, 'Geez, just shag the guy already.'"

"It would save me the humiliation of begging." But he didn't laugh or look amused when her head dipped toward his chest. His muscles bunched under her curling fingers.

He let her set the pace and it was intoxicating. The power went straight to her head. Okay, it overpowered a couple of other areas too. When he let go of the covers she guided his hands to the headboard. Then she leaned in close to his ear and whispered, "Let's see if this can compete with sun and sand."

The heat from his skin released the scent of citrus into the air. She dipped her head. Straight to the part of him pleading for attention. His legs parted to give her access and she stroked and cradled. Her tongue swirled. A low moan poured into the air. She'd never done this before. Ever. Hadn't wanted to get this close to any man. Underneath her fingers, his muscles tensed, his back bowed. She discovered the power to make him beg and she didn't hesitate to use it.

She lapped at him. Took more of him in until the tip of his erection touched the back of her throat. His hands gripped her head and guided her. Her tongue, her hands, pulled the groans out of his throat.

Words came out of his mouth, loud enough to get her attention. Commanding enough to make her listen. Explicit enough to excite.

She tightened her grip. Increased the rhythm. Did all the things he demanded.

Then he begged.

For more.

For harder.

And then he begged her to stop.

They met in the middle space between them. Their tongues engaged, happy to explore the warmth and welcome. When the time came he scrambled for his pants and the condoms stashed there. The heat of his hands molded her heavy breasts. She settled over top of his hips and lowered herself down.

"Look at me." His hands gripped her hips. Momentum built. She was mesmerized by the sight of him. All corded muscle, skin sleek with sweat, eyes open. She rushed toward the edge of the cliff and jumped.

Chapter Eight

Sophie rued the dawning of a new week. They'd spent a quiet Sunday recuperating, watching movies, talking, planning. But Monday came and she was forced to spend the day at her clinic. New Year's Eve day was always a gong show. Added to this year's chaos, word of Marnie's death had spread on the street. Her staff posted arrangement notices, none of which had been finalized, for all the people asking. By 9:30 Sophie's head was aching.

The morning was business as usual. They tried to accommodate as many people as possible, whether they had an appointment or not. If they were turned away chances were they wouldn't be back. Part of Sophie's mandate was to work with the ebb and flow of the area's transient lifestyle. Her job was to treat people. Not create more problems.

But all of a sudden she couldn't do it. Couldn't witness another single second of someone else's pain. Hers was too overwhelming. The door whispered shut behind her. She pressed her shoulders against the hard wood surface.

Silence.

She inhaled the scent of patchouli she used to combat stress. There was a bookshelf on the left wall with her mp3 docking station. This morning she'd left it on shuffle. Adele was "Rolling In The Deep." Her shoulders relaxed. Until a soft knock made her sigh. She checked her watch. What had it been? Five seconds?

She pulled open the door to see her receptionist's worried face. When she didn't say anything Sophie's radar went off. She retreated behind her cluttered desk and dropped into her chair. "What's wrong?"

Peggy peeked back out the door before stepping in and closing it. She regarded Sophie. "Liam's here."

Sophie stared at her. "What?"

"He's insisting on seeing you." Peggy was very protective. She was also a no-nonsense kind of woman who didn't take any flak from anyone. To see her flustered shook Sophie out of her shock.

She rearranged papers on her desk, bought herself some time. What the hell was he doing here? Why now? Why today? She wanted to refuse to see him but it was a childish thought. It implied she still cared. It wasn't the case. Not anymore. And there was the little matter of finding out what he knew of Jason Drummond's plans. "Show him in."

Peggy crossed her arms. "Not exactly the solution I had in mind."

"Me, either. But I actually need to talk to him."

Peggy pursed her lips in disapproval.

Sophie sighed. "Give us five minutes. If he's still here, then we'll throw him out."

Peggy gave her a gleeful thumbs up and slipped out. Sophie collapsed back into her chair and prepared to deal with the guy who'd taken another woman with him on their honeymoon. The door opened once again and Peggy ushered Liam in with a scowl. She made a point of leaving the door wide open.

With his hair cut close to his head, his tall lean runner's body tense, Liam Gallagher crossed her threshold. "Sophie. It's good to see you."

Sophie ignored his greeting. "You have five minutes. Make the most of them."

Instead Liam chose to arrange his long frame into the chair across from her. He tucked his jacket around him, crossed a leg over a knee. His smile was blinding and nervous. Everything about him matched from his tie to his socks. Sophie raised a brow before giving her watch an exaggerated glance.

He had the grace to tone down the smile. "I heard about Marnie. I'm sorry."

The word bullshit came to mind. He didn't look the least bit sorry. "How sweet of you. I know how much you cared for her."

"I'm here because I care about you."

It was rude and snarky but it made her day to laugh straight at him, to mock his fake sympathy. "Why don't you get to the part where you give me Drummond's message?"

"He didn't send me."

"Really?"

"I volunteered to come."

"Ah."

He leaned forward, all pretense gone. "You need to back off."

"Goodbye, Liam." She picked up a patient folder and rose to her feet.

He did the same. "I'm serious. He's pumping me for information about you. For details. He's fishing for anything he can get on you."

She put her hand over her heart. "And being the

upstanding citizen you are, and seeing how you care for me, I'm sure you've explained how I'm none of his fucking business."

Deep lines appeared around his mouth. He no longer smiled or worked to cajole. "Whatever you're doing to antagonize him, you need to drop it."

"I have no intention of giving him that kind of satisfaction." Which sounded both pissy and prissy, but she couldn't and wouldn't help it.

He threw up his hands. "How could I forget? You don't take advice. Especially if it interferes with your plans for saving the world."

"I get we don't have the same agenda. And I'm done apologizing to you for focusing on the things that matter to me." She stabbed a finger into her chest.

He invaded her space. She resisted the urge to back up. "He's collecting all the information he can about you. How you practice. Your philosophies. Your finances. Your associates. What you do outside of work. You name it he's asking it."

She laid a hand against his chest and pushed him back. "I don't keep secrets. He can ask whatever he likes."

Liam sneered. "How about Caleb Quinn? Is his life an open book too? Are you sure there are no skeletons in his closet?"

She shut her mouth and left it closed. She didn't know and she sure as hell wasn't going there with him.

"How much does he matter to you?" Liam grabbed her hand and tugged her closer. "I don't know what Marnie did to screw things up this time, but you need to let whatever it is go. The Drummonds aren't people you want to piss off. Jason's doing his best to discredit

Quinn any and everywhere. You don't need him coming after you too."

Her heart stuttered over his mention of Caleb. "What do you mean he's trying to discredit Caleb?"

"If that's the part that worries you, you're not listening. You're going to go down with him if you don't distance yourself."

She yanked her hand free. "As usual, you're timing leaves a lot to be desired. He's already busy doing the most damage he can. So, too little; too late."

He blocked her path when she went to shove past. "What's that supposed mean?"

Why the hell shouldn't she tell him? "This building. My clinic? He bought it and he's evicting us."

"What?"

"You heard me. Now get out. I don't want or need your belated advice."

He grabbed for her arms. "All the more reason to listen to what I have to say. He's not going to stop there. Not if you keep poking at him."

"Or maybe I'll just get a bigger stick."

He gave her a shake. "For once in your life. Back. Down."

She pushed away from him. "I can't."

"Sophie." He pulled her back in, stepped closer until they were nose to nose. His hands moved to frame her face. "I care about you. I'm sorry I hurt you, more sorry than I can say. Don't let our past be the reason you ignore what I'm saying."

"I'm not. I don't expect you to understand why this is so important to me." Not the way Caleb did. She put her hands over his. She no longer cared what his agenda was in coming to see her. What he stood to gain. It didn't matter to her anymore. "Goodbye, Liam."

Someone cleared their throat and she looked past Liam expecting to see Peggy. Caleb stood in the doorway with her. Peggy planted her hands on her hips. "Sorry to interrupt. But it's been five minutes."

"No, it's all right." Sophie stepped back from Liam. A blush of heat crept up her throat. "Liam was leaving."

Peggy shook her head and walked away. The two men rooted their feet to the floor. Even though they were roughly the same height, same weight, and had the same objective, Liam was outmatched. And outclassed.

"Caleb this is Liam Gallagher. Liam. Caleb Quinn." Introductions done she retreated to the space behind her desk.

The two men made no effort to shake hands. Caleb stepped into her office and the space shrunk.

Sophie motioned at Liam. "Thanks for stopping by and offering your condolences."

Liam ignored her, instead he glared at Caleb. "You'd better have one hell of an ace up your sleeve."

"I can handle Drummond."

"I could care less what happens to you, Quinn. My concern is Sophie."

Caleb's face gave nothing away. The heat was in the clenching and unclenching of his hands. The stiffening of his shoulders. "A little late for concern, don't you think?"

Seriously?

Her head ached. Her heart hurt. She was embarrassed for no good reason. She gripped the back of her chair and shoved it toward her desk. "Okay, you know what? I'm not up for a pissing contest today."

Caleb's hot gaze turned on her but he spoke to Liam. "I have it under control."

"Are you sure?" Liam demanded.

"Meaning?" countered Caleb.

Liam addressed his answer to Sophie. "He found out about your deal with Forrester Pharmaceuticals."

Sophie frowned. "So?"

"Are you so blinded by the cause you don't see how it might look to the general public?" Liam's tone softened, turned pleading. "This battle isn't worth the cost to your reputation."

Sophie narrowed her eyes. "How did he find out?"

Liam looked away. Ran a hand over his mouth. Shook his head. "He's not going to stop. He's crazy over this situation. You need to back down."

She slapped her hands down on her desk. "How did he find out, Liam?"

"I can't afford not to do business with him, Sophie."

Caleb turned away in disgust. Sophie kept her face neutral. Now she knew what was in it for him. Liam headed for the door. He stopped in the doorway. "This project has been in the works for months. Luck put me in his path. But he still knew to come to me, to make use of our connection. He's done his homework. Under the money and the gloss, he's one scary son of a bitch. You need to remember that."

The rest of his warning fell short. Scary was for movies and haunted houses. Her sister was dead because of Jason Drummond. A man who made his own rules, one who figured he was above it all, a human bulldozer. Scary? He was a whole other breed of monster.

****

Everything in Caleb seethed. She'd all but kissed the selfish son of a bitch. Deal? What kind of deal were they talking about? The futility of their situation fueled his burning need to walk away. To call retreat. Raise the white flag.

He needed space. And a reality check. He shoved his fists into his pants pocket. "Do I even want to know what deal he's talking about?"

"It's nothing out of the ordinary." She kept busy straightening objects and papers on her desk. Classic evasion tactics and it frustrated the hell out of him.

He didn't say a word. He let the silence settle in around them.

She sighed. "I'm consulting on market research regarding an experimental therapy for addiction to a very specific type of narcotic. Nothing unethical."

"Experimental."

"Yes."

"For which you receive a fee."

"And that's public knowledge." She dropped the gathered papers down on her desk.

"Expect the public doesn't generally go asking."

She leveled a look at him. "Your point?"

"You know the point. What happens when it becomes public knowledge? When John Doe and Jane Smith start trading gossip over the hedge in suburbia and the main topic of conversation is you and your *experimental therapies*? When they're fed the story you're getting paid to add more controversy to an already volatile situation? Think about your reputation."

"It's the right kind of treatment for the problems

we see here." Her hands landed on her hips, the fire back in her eyes.

"It doesn't matter to people who never see the need for it. People who have no experience with addiction. Unless you count gravy boats and socket wrenches. Jason is going to paint you as a radical. He's going to try and use this information to discredit you."

"He can't discredit me if I've done nothing wrong."

Was she for real? "How can you be so naïve? He's going to tear your reputation to shreds. The radical doctor whose mentally ill, drug addicted sister was murdered in a squalid downtown hotel room. Every time your name comes up it will be associated with the lovely trifecta of booze, drugs, and criminal activity. You'll never get another dollar in funding. Once he kicks you out of this building he'll make sure no one else is interested in leasing you space."

She said nothing. Hurt brought a sheen to her lovely eyes. The fight ebbed out of her. The energy. The precious spark giving her life. It was in the slump of her shoulders, the shadows under her eyes, the wringing of her hands. She was done, caving in on herself. Giving too much. Expecting nothing. It had to stop.

He had to stop her.

"It's time for you to distance yourself. From now on I'll deal with Drummond. I'll make the arrangements, see this through. But you? You are done with this."

A hint of yesterday's Sophie surfaced. "You don't get to decide for me."

"Yeah, I do. Gallagher's right. This isn't worth the

fallout." He swallowed back the flare of guilt. The pain of disappointing her stabbed at him, but fear was a great motivator. And he had plenty of it. For her. "I'll finalize the legalities with Jason over child support. The rest of it is for the police. It's done. We're done. I'll be in touch in a couple of days."

He didn't wait to hear her answer, but headed through her office door. *Coward.* It was a whisper in his ear. He shook it off. After tonight was done, he'd talk to her. Explain. If she still wanted to slap him down, fine. He could live with leaving her if it meant salvaging her reputation. Her safety. Her life.

He walked through the crammed clinic. The high of doing the right thing lasted until he hit the street. His steps slowed the further he walked. Each inhalation of winter air stabbed at his lungs. He took a steady breath. It did nothing to ease the ache in his chest. He braced against what he had to do and prepared to meet a friend for lunch, the crushing weight of choice and sacrifice killing his appetite. Then it was party time.

Chapter Nine

Sophie wasn't an idiot, contrary to popular belief. She rummaged in her clutch for her gilt-edged invitation. The tuxedoed woman guarding the entrance checked her name against the list on her clipboard and nodded. Caleb wasn't the only one with friends in high places. If he was in attendance, so was she. Someone had to make sure he didn't sacrifice himself at the altar of stupidity.

She smoothed a hand over her hip, the material covering them like gloss on lips. The dress fit a little snugger than she remembered. A couple of years out of date, it had none of the naughty goddess appeal of the little black dress she'd bought to torture Caleb with on Christmas Eve. But it provided more coverage. She wasn't out to attract attention. Going glam wasn't the way to crash this glitzy North Shore bash.

The whole place flickered with hundreds of little outside lights. Inside the lighting was subdued but oh-so-carefully charming. 13,000 square feet of house built on prime waterfront real estate. Ocean views meant lots of windows. Yards of glass. All without a smudge. Like the house in the Twilight movies. Go figure.

Inside she spotted an Emily Carr on one interior wall and a still life of Mary Pratt's on another. Decadent arrangements of blood red hydrangea and creamy white roses dripped from silver urns. Live music played in the background, soft and passive. Surfaces gleamed, conversation flowed, and jewels sparkled. Guests mingled around the pièce de résistance. Sophie figured it was more phallic symbol than Christmas tree.

Waiters in spotless white button-down shirts and jet black pants mingled with trays of canapés and wine. Gowned women and tuxedoed men mingled, plates and drink glasses in hand. Sophie snagged a glass off a tray, more to have something in her hand than any urge to drink. Her stomach revolted at the very idea. Her objective? Find Caleb. They'd figure out the rest later.

Proof the universe provided was in the convenient parting of a group of people. There he stood looking gorgeous in black tie parlaying with the rich and famous. Was there ever any doubt? He fit in here, polished, at ease, surrounded by his peers. He smiled, lifted his glass at a quip while she stood alone, the proverbial cheese.

A woman squeezed in beside him and he shifted to make room for her, lent his cheek for a kiss. She threaded her arm through his, a smile the size of Queen Charlotte Sound lighting up her face. Strapless, short red stretch left miles of tanned skin to appreciate.

Tiffany.

Like the blue box with the white ribbon she begged to be unwrapped. Sophie had gotten it wrong. So wrong. Caleb wasn't here to avenge anything. Jealousy snaked its way down to her fingers. They wrapped around her clutch, crushing the soft fabric until she could separate out its meager contents. Then she pictured them wrapped around a set of something a whole lot more delicate. And Caleb's face twisted in pain.

She spun around intending to leave only to come up short.

"Doctor Monroe, I don't remember seeing your name on the guest list." Jason Drummond put a hand on her elbow holding her in place. She wanted to slap the hoity look off his face. He tsked. "Don't be too upset with Caleb. His attention span is short and Tiffany is a favorite of his."

Her heart stopped. Not because she believed him, but because she didn't. It was his leer. He had mean in his eyes as Marnie would say. She indulged in a mouthful of wine to buy a couple of seconds to calm the hell down. To think. To trust.

"Nothing to say, Dr. Monroe?"

"At least she's age appropriate." She stared straight at him. Took in his hard eyes, the twelve inches of height he had on her, the eighty plus pounds. "What's your excuse?"

She winced, the pressure on her elbow increasing. There would be bruises there in the morning. "You might remember you're here on my sufferance. The second I cease to find you amusing I'll have you thrown out. You need to ask yourself if your reputation can handle being tossed out onto the street."

The laughter bubbled out of her, she couldn't help it. The man's arrogance knew no bounds. "You do not want to go down the reputation road with me."

He tugged her close, smiled like he was preparing to share a naughty secret. "Then again maybe I do."

She tried to yank her arm back. It did no good. He was stronger than her.

"Seeing as you're just a different kind of whore."

His breath grazed her cheek, stinking of alcohol and tobacco. "I'm sure you can spread your legs with the best of them."

She recoiled, repulsed. Ready to do battle.

"There you are." Caleb's arm wrapped around her waist and tugged. Jason had no choice. He let her go. At first glance, Caleb's grin was easy. Second glance, not so much. He lowered his head and kissed her on the lips. Slow, warm, with a bit of warning mixed in.

Jason let a little of his façade slip. He gestured at Caleb. "The two of you can show yourselves out."

Caleb blocked his exit. "You and I need to talk."

"Tonight is for celebrating the future. Progress. Moving forward. As neither of you seem to be fans of the program, you can leave. Immediately." He snagged a glass of wine off a passing tray and toasted in their direction.

Caleb didn't budge. "I spoke to Kimberley McKay today. She doesn't send her regards by the way."

Alerted Sophie searched his face. Who the hell was Kimberley McKay?

Jason's astonishment was temporary. Mute hatred came next, casting a little black venomous cloud over the three of them.

Caleb nodded at Sophie, a gleam of triumph in his serious eyes. "We went to school together. The three of us. You'd like her. Right now she's on maternity leave from her job as an addictions counselor on the East Coast."

Jason affected a bored look while a very unattractive red stained his cheeks. "I'm glad to hear she's doing well. She suffered from her share of problems. Delusions being one of them if I remember correctly."

"I guess a quarter of a million dollars buys a lot of therapy. Now I think it's time to take this conversation elsewhere, don't you?"

His lips thinned and he held out his hand. "After you."

Sophie grabbed for Caleb's hand. "Don't."

He gave her fingers a squeeze. "It'll be fine."

Jason spread his hands. "I'm a little pressed for time, so…"

"This will just take a second." Caleb stepped in front of Sophie. "Go home, Sophie. Please."

Not on your life, Caleb Quinn. It was going to take a hell of a lot longer than *a few seconds* to convince her to leave. "Don't worry about me. I'll find Tiffany. We'll chat. A cat fight might be just the thing this dull bash needs."

"Sophie—"

"Caleb," demanded Jason.

"I'm right behind you." He turned back to Sophie. "I know what I'm doing."

She searched his face. "It's what you're sacrificing that worries me."

"I'm not."

She didn't believe him. "Well, be careful doing whatever it is you're not doing."

Sophie reached up and pulled his head down. Her mouth opened over his and discretion wasn't her aim. If Tiffany was watching she wanted her to get the message. Caleb Quinn was hers. "I'm still really pissed at you."

"Noted." On a parting smile he followed her sister's murderer out of the room.

She'd be waiting. Patience was a virtue. The only one she could claim. And she took care of her own. Otherwise Marnie would haunt her for the rest of her days.

****

Caleb inspected Jason's private sanctum. Unlike his corporate office space it was steeped in wood paneling. Upholstered chairs flanked a mammoth black walnut desk. Photos hung on the walls. But unlike Sophie's most of these showed Jason tagging big game, reeling in big fish, or shaking hands with big celebrities. Draperies hung from rods, awards lined shelves. Even in the midst of all the fuss the man stood out. But where everyone else saw Prince Charming he saw a narcissist and a manipulator. And so much worse.

"You can't prove anything." Jason turned from his overly casual contemplation of the view.

"Maybe that's not what this is about."

"Spare me the rhetoric and get to your point. In case you haven't noticed I'm kind of busy." He went to his desk and poured a drink.

Caleb nodded at his glass. "It's a rare thing to see you without a drink in your hand these days."

"And here I was under the impression you didn't care."

Caleb crossed his arms. "Did you really think you'd get away with it?"

"This is getting tedious." He swilled back a mouthful of scotch. "Get away with what? I have no idea what you're talking about."

"To which I say bullshit. Now, I have a few requests." Caleb shook his head. "Should you refuse to grant these requests I'm going to make your life hell."

Jason snorted out a laugh. "Something we both know you don't have the balls for."

"It's not too late for you to do the right thing."

"By a lying, cheating whore? I don't think so."

"She's the mother of your child."

"I don't have a child. When I do? He'll come from quality and he'll be raised in the appropriate manner."

"Like you were?"

"Again, point? Since you don't have one, get the hell out of my house and take the good doctor with you."

"My point? Let's see. You pay for sex. You have them dress like schoolgirls. Then you pay them off. When people get in your way you have them murdered."

"And I'm guessing if you could prove it we wouldn't be having this conversation."

"You might be surprised."

"I don't think so."

"Then fuck you for being stupid because here's how it's going to work. You will pay child support. You're going to gift Sophie the building you bought out from under her. While you're at it, you're also going to arrange to fund 100 low income apartments in the Downtown Eastside."

"And why the hell would I do all that?" His scorn paired well with his flat eyes.

"The idea there's no such thing as bad publicity may apply to billionaire party girls, but I don't think it applies to you." Caleb flipped open his cell phone and pulled up the photo he'd taken of the bald man lurking downstairs at the party. The one with the swastika tattoo blotted out by a bad makeup job. He turned it around to show Jason. "He's one of yours. Don't bother denying it. He was there the night you found us at the Empress. And he was at the Balmoral the night Marnie was killed. I saw him."

Jason remained silent.

Caleb tilted his head. "Nothing to say."

Jason shrugged, spread his hands. "So what? I'm hardly responsible for where my employees land on their off time."

He shoved his phone back into his pocket. "You're right, of course. I can't prove anything."

Jason dropped down into his overstuffed desk chair. "Then I guess there's nothing left except for you to get the hell out of my house."

Caleb leaned over and planted his fists on the front of the desk. "Then again, I don't need proof to ruin you. All I need to do is whisper in the ear of the right people. Rumor and ruin."

"But whose ruin?"

"In the interest of full disclosure I'll inform you I'm hiring a private investigator to track your moves. Consider me your version of a restraining order. Do not come near Sophie or Kellie and Quinn again." Caleb pulled a stack of papers from the inside pocket of his tuxedo. He tossed them on the desk. "I've marked all the places requiring your signature."

"You're going to regret this." The gloss he showed the world slipped, his glamor spell broken. Through the cracks the cost of living two lives showed on his face.

"You had sex with an eighteen year old girl. You threw her and your unborn child out into the street." He pushed all the disgust churning in his gut into his next words. "You're a rapist—"

"Watch it, Caleb."

"I won't regret a thing."

"You're suffering from an inflated opinion of your abilities. There's nothing to prove. And furthermore, I'm going to see to it you lose your license to practice law."

Caleb reached over and smoothed out the folded sheaf of papers. "You're free to do whatever you like. After you sign these."

"Here's what I think of your request." He grabbed them and ripped them in two. He tossed them back on the desk with a laugh. "Fuck *you* for being stupid."

"Big mistake. And yet I'm not surprised."

"Get out."

"Well, that's it then. Seems you've bested me." Caleb prepared to leave but paused with his hand on the doorknob. He made a show of deep thought, added in a fake frown. "I haven't seen Kristine tonight?"

Jason's brows drew together at the sudden change in topic. "She's feeling under the weather but she'll put in an appearance when I make my announcement."

"Strange. She was fine today at lunch. Maybe she heard something that didn't agree with her." Caleb feigned surprise. He lifted a shoulder, let it drop and allowed a small smile. "Might be wise to hold off making any kind of announcement for the foreseeable future. It would be embarrassing to have to withdraw. I'll see you in my office Wednesday morning, 10:00 o'clock. Bring your lawyer. And your wallet."

He closed the door behind him. Bile burned its way up his throat. A second later the door gave a slight shudder. He breathed in deep at the sound of shattering glass. He remembered the tears from lunch, the heated words, the heartbreak. Kristine's promise to stay away tonight. No matter what he thought of Jason, his wife was a friend and she was hurting now because of him. He wondered if a wiser man would have done better. There was no lightness of being. No sense of having done the right thing. Only guilt.

****

Sophie turned at the gentle tap to her shoulder. Surprise made her clumsy and a couple of drops dribbled over from her glass onto her fingers. She switched hands, licked the spill away. All in an "Oh, shit," kind of daze. Undoubtedly a faux pas in front of royalty. She recognized her, of course. The glossy photos of the society pages failed to do her pale perfection justice. Her gown was couture, some crepe-y blue piece complete with a black pearl choker necklace and drop down pearl earrings. The only thing missing was the tiara.

Great.

"Dr. Monroe?"

"Yes."

"I'm Kristine Drummond." The fabled Novo Yellow diamond engagement ring glittered from its perch on her ring finger, her outstretched hand waiting. "Caleb and I are…ah…friends. He mentioned you at lunch today."

"Ms. Drummond." Sophie's eyes narrowed. What the frack? Lunch? She called up a smile and clasped Kristine's cool fingers. "I'm sorry you were so short of topics you were reduced to discussing me."

"Please, call me Kristine." Her smile never wavered, but her tone held a note of pain and her absolute perfection hid an alarming pallor. Kristine

194

Drummond broke eye contact and ran a hand over her stomach. "He seems to have left you all alone. Caleb isn't known for his bad manners."

What was she supposed to say? *He's busy accusing your husband of murder.* She sipped from her glass of warm white wine. Her eyes strayed to the door. No sign of Caleb.

"I'm sure he'll be back soon," Sophie insisted.

"In the meantime let me show you around." Despite her ashen complexion her face shimmered with a dew of sweat. She dabbed at the skin over her upper lip.

"I'm sure you have more important things to do than drag me around. I'm quite content observing, thank you for the offer." Sophie tilted her head, her doctor instincts tingling. "Are you okay?"

"I'm fine." She waved off Sophie's question and leaned in. "But I'm dying to know more about you. You're not Caleb's usual type."

Sophie couldn't have stopped her eye roll to save her life. "So everyone keeps saying."

A smile lifted her lips but failed to reach her eyes. "You're a vast improvement, believe me."

Why should she? She was Jason Drummond's wife. How much did she know? How much had she ignored? Sophie wasn't about to trust her.

"Caleb mentioned you're in need of donations. I insist you let me take you on the deep pockets tour." Her fingers were a soft touch on the back of Sophie's arm, her quiet breath warm against her ear, her tone insistent. It suggested compliance was mandatory. "We'll likely run into Caleb as we make the rounds."

The very last person Sophie wanted to spend time

with was Jason Drummond's wife. But she was beginning to worry about Caleb. Maybe a tour was a chance to check things out and ask a few questions.

They left the main room with its windows and low lighting, its crush of people. The next room was less populated. Still no Caleb. A group shifted to include them. Kristine tried to guide her past but was forced to stop and make introductions. Small talk passed back and forth from glossed lips and smiling mouths. The same line of conversation she'd engaged in all night.

"A doctor?"

"Yes."

"What's your specialty?"

"I'm a family physician."

"How nice. Where do you practice?"

"The Downtown Eastside."

"Oh. Well, good for you."

Awkward silence and then the conversation shifted to more appropriate topics like the weather. Sophie supplied more answers to pat questions and concentrated on observing. Kristine Drummond should have been in her element, enjoying the party, anticipating her husband's big announcement. But like day-old champagne her performance was flat.

She tested a theory. "Excuse me, I see a friend."

Sophie stepped to the side. So did Kristine. Sophie smiled. So did Kristine. She placed a hand on Sophie's arm. To hold her in place? A warning not to go anywhere?

Was she morphing into a suspicious wreck?

Or was Kristine Drummond stalking her. A waiter paused and offered his tray of appetizers for their perusal, a selection of tiny tarts and wild salmon skewers. Her new best friend stifled a gag. A discreet hand over pursed lips. Mere seconds of reaction. But when added to the waxiness of her skin, the dark circles showing under the carefully applied makeup? A paranoid notion formed and her tired brain kneaded it into probability.

She forced her eyes to blink, her hands to still. It was ridiculous. And none of her business. But the awful possibility plowed a furrow of alarm. She did another futile check for Caleb. How long had he been gone?

A man approached Kristine and whispered in her ear. She made excuses on their behalf. Once again Sophie's arm was in her grasp and they were on the move.

Sophie pulled her arm out of Kristine's hold. "I think this is where you and I part company."

Kristine spared her a half-hearted smile but a plea lurked in her eyes. "Tonight my husband expects me to play the role of the Good Wife, despite the fact he…I don't expect you to understand my motives but I hope you'll recognize my need for answers."

She was not going down this rutted, gnarly track of road with Drummond's wife. "Feel free to talk to someone—anyone—else."

Kristine glanced around before whispering, "Please. I know you have them to give. Help me understand."

"I'm not that kind of doctor." And she was out of patience.

Kristine's fingers tightened around her arm, her nails bit into her skin. "I can get your clinic back for you."

"Was there anything he didn't tell you?" Sophie

raised her eyebrows and glanced down at her arm.

Kristine let go at once. "As I said, we're friends."

"You get one shot at an explanation."

Kristine blew out a soft breath. "Not here."

Sophie laughed, looked away. Back again. "What makes you think I'm going to follow you anywhere?"

"You can't expect me to discuss this in the middle of a ball."

"Your call." She turned to walk away.

"Perhaps I was wrong and you really are just using him. Same as all the rest."

Her taunt hit its mark. Every muscle tensed. She turned back. "What's that supposed to mean."

"You seem perfectly willing to let Caleb take all the risks."

Everything in her went cold. She ignored the insult. "If Caleb's in trouble, so help me…"

Kristine's chin went up. "Jason would never hurt Caleb."

Sophie closed in. "Are you really that delusional?"

"Come with me and find out."

One inch closer. Then two. She was close enough to count the drops of sweat dotting her hairline. "If anything happens to Caleb I will spend the rest of my life making sure you pay."

"I'm already paying plenty." Kristine Drummond held out her hand. "This way."

They snaked their way through the knots of people toward a side door. It led into a smaller room, a kind of lady's library. Lined with books, it held a small desk flanked by two sleek chairs. The same stunning view showed outside the vast window. Behind her the door closed on a soft click.

"Can I get you a drink?"

"Where's Caleb?" Sophie demanded.

Kristine threw her hands into the air. "My guess? Off accusing Jason of God knows what."

"We have to find him."

Kristine gave her a look before closing her eyes and pressing at the spot in the middle of her forehead. "Now's not the time to go looking."

And didn't those words scare the crap out of her. "I disagree."

"Why don't we both sit down?"

"I don't believe I will."

"Please," Kristine asked, a hitch in her breathing. Once again her hand went to her stomach as she closed her eyes for a second.

Against her will Sophie's concern spiked. "Are you sure you're all right?"

"Never better." Kristine sank into one of the chairs at the desk.

Concerned Sophie crossed the small room. "How far along are you?"

Kristine shrugged then reached for the pitcher and a glass from a mirrored tray. "Exactly twelve weeks."

"Any complications?" Sophie confiscated both items and poured her a glass of water. Handed it to her.

Kristine's laugh was low and mocking. "Are you seriously asking me that question?"

"I mean, physically?"

She took a cautious sip of water. "Morning sickness, nothing out of the ordinary."

"Have you eaten today?"

"Well, I was looking forward to lunch with a friend, but over the course of our conversation I lost my appetite."

"Nothing since then?" She picked up the other woman's hand, turned it over, placed her first two fingers on the outside of Kristine's wrist. She counted, took note of her respirations.

"No." Kristine shook her head.

Sophie needed to find Caleb. "I'll go find you something to eat and have it sent back here for you. I want you to eat as much as you possibly can. Tomorrow you need to go see your doctor."

"There's no need for you to go to any trouble." She picked up the phone from the desk and placed an order. Wealth did have its privileges. "Besides, you were about to tell me what's going on."

She hedged. "Perhaps you need to talk to your husband."

"As I'm currently not speaking to him, it might prove difficult."

"I'm not the one you should be asking."

"You promised me answers."

"And as a doctor, I'm prescribing rest. Not more stress."

"Did you know I'm worth millions?" She set her glass down. Folded her hands in her lap.

"Is there anyone who doesn't?" Sophie perched on the edge of the seat across from her.

"It's why I can get your clinic back for you."

Sophie shifted in her chair. She didn't want to hear it. She didn't want to sympathize with a woman who hadn't walked out the minute she'd heard her husband was a monster.

Kristine started drawing little circles on the polished desk. "I love my husband. I thought he loved me. Turns out he loves my money more. We've been married for five years and right from the start I wanted a child. But Jason always had an excuse for waiting. I filled my life with the things that mattered to him. That didn't mean I wasn't happy. I was. Then six months ago he changed his mind. I was overjoyed."

Sophie didn't know what to say and worse she couldn't predict how much Caleb had told her and what he had left out.

"Finally, a baby. And today I find out he's already fathered a child." She stopped, bit her lip, composed herself.

"This isn't doing you any good. Why don't we find you a place to stay for the night? You shouldn't stay here. This whole situation is too upsetting. You need your rest. See your doctor tomorrow. Your health is the most important thing right now."

Kristine ignored her. "And the mother is an eighteen year old girl he bought and paid for with my money." Her fist hit the desk.

Sophie jumped. Okay, she knew a bit more than Sophie expected.

"I come from self-made money. You've heard of Lincoln Lumber? Of course you have. Everyone knows my granddaddy is as proud of his humble beginnings as he is of his millions. My people are hardworking, upstanding citizens still waiting for their first Order of Canada, first lieutenant governor posting, and first appointment to a useless Senate. Unlike my husband's family who hold claim to all those achievements. Unfortunately for them you still need money to pull off their kind of private land deals. And it's Lincoln money that makes them possible."

Sophie didn't know what to say. Staying with someone who doesn't love you, who's incapable of loving you…

It's not other's decisions that matter, it's your own.

She almost smiled. Maybe life with Marnie had managed to teach her something after all.

"What are you going to do?" asked Sophie.

Kristine dipped her head. "I have no idea beyond the obvious. I know I have to leave. But at a time of my choosing. First and foremost I'll protect my family's interests. I need more information."

"What makes you think I'll tell you anything new?" Sophie held up a hand. "For clarity's sake, I want to make it clear I'm not interested in your money or any other incentive plan you might dream up."

"All right. An appeal woman to woman. What kind of monster am I married to?"

"Are you asking because you're interested in damage control? Or are you worried for your safety?"

"If it's a little of both?"

"I'm not a spin doctor. I don't cure deceit or stitch reputations back together."

"You don't pull any punches, do you?"

"And I can't help but think the less you know the better. The duped wife. Sympathy would be yours for the taking."

"A single incident of infidelity can be forgiven. Her age and the fact there's a child makes this situation infinitely more complicated." She placed a hand on her stomach. "But no matter what I do, this child will be a Drummond. Jason will always be his father. There's no escaping it. Or him. From now on what I do? I do in the interest of protecting my child. So, I'm going to ask you again. How much more is there to it?"

There was no time to explain. The door opened and the man who'd been with Jason in her apartment stepped inside. He closed the door and stood with his hands crossed in front of him. "Jason wants to see you."

Kristine straightened. Sophie had to admire her ability to call up haughty on command. Like all she had to do was raise the eyebrow of death and the peasants cowered before her. "You can tell my husband I'm unavailable for the foreseeable future."

Except this guy hadn't gotten the royal memo. His expression remained neutral, his stance wide. He pulled out his phone, made a call, and stuffed it back in his pocket. Oh yeah, and he made sure to shift his coat to the side and hook his suit jacket back behind his gun holster. "He'd prefer it if you came now."

Kristine froze.

Sophie put a hand on her arm, more to gauge a possible collapse than in warning. Because hell no was she going anywhere with this guy. She had vocal cords and she wasn't afraid to use them. "I'm not going anywhere. You can tell your boss if he wants to see me he'll have to come to me."

He reached back and Sophie flinched, but all he did was turn the doorknob and push it open. For a moment she thought he was actually going to go get Drummond. Instead, another man stepped into the room, his companion from the Empress. The one who'd walked out of the Balmoral. The one who'd killed her sister.

Her heart hammered out a warning. She knew they were in trouble. Big trouble. The other man's eyes remained neutral along with his expression. He was here to do a job with no vested interest in doing more than he was bid. The skinhead's tattoos marked him as a zealot and worse. A smirk lifted the corners of his lips. His posture read arrogant from his pushed back shoulders to his loose fists. Anticipation blazed in his eyes.

"Ladies, after you." He gave a slight bow, held out a polite hand.

"What are you going to do? Shoot us? In the middle of a party?" God, she hoped not, but bravado was the only defense she had handy.

"Nope." He strolled over and pried the tiny party-sized purse out from underneath her arm. Her keys landed on the floor and her lip gloss rolled into a corner. He stuffed her phone in a pocket and tossed her clutch to the floor. He pulled out his own phone. When he found what he was looking for he leaned in to share it with her. She refused to engage and he nudged her, like they were best friends and she needed to have a look. Another nudge. Harder this time. She glanced down.

Her house. Next photo: Caleb coming up her walk. One of her. Next: Kellie pushing Quinn in the stroller they'd borrowed. Another picture of Kellie. Kellie again. She held herself still. Her brain flinched then stalled, deprived of air. She sucked in a breath. Kellie's silhouette through her front window.

"Very pretty. Always thought so." The smile, and his triumph, were in his voice. "All tucked in for the night. Safe. For now."

Sophie lifted her head. What was there to say? To do? She turned to Kristine, who watched with a hand pressed against her mouth, disbelieving. They stared at each other. Sophie nodded. Then they turned and walked through another side door into an empty hallway.

****

Caleb searched for Sophie among the many guests. It was a packed house. He checked his watch. Again. It was 11:15 pm. Still more guests arrived creating an ebb and flow of people. Friends and acquaintances greeted each other, moved on. People gathered around the bar areas set up at various stations. Wait staff roamed with trays. Jewels glittered, laughter trilled, music serenaded them.

But no Sophie. He knew in his gut she wouldn't leave without him. Too stubborn. Too invested in the outcome.

A waiter paused beside him, he shook his head. His stomach churned, but it wasn't hunger. It was concern. Or something a few levels above it. He never should have left her alone.

He spotted Tiffany across the room. She was snuggled up against another acquaintance of theirs. He headed in their direction.

"Tiffany, Evan."

They exchanged pleasantries. He ignored Tiffany's pout.

"Have you seen Dr. Monroe?"

"Who?"

He didn't have the patience to deal with her shallow bitchiness. He didn't care if her uncle was a managing partner. "It's important."

She snuggled closer to Evan. "She left with Kristine."

Caleb froze. "Kristine's here?"

Tiffany looked at him like he was crazy. "It's kind

of her party."

"I was under the impression she wasn't feeling well."

"She seemed fine to me." She shrugged and turned away.

"Thanks." He patted Evan's shoulder in sympathy. "Take care."

Worst case scenarios danced through his mind like poisoned sugar plums. He wove a path through the chatter. Jason didn't know Kristine was at the party. Good thing or bad thing? Or a lie? What was Sophie doing with Kristine? And why couldn't he find either of them?

A crush of people parted and he stepped into their midst. He mumbled a few words of small talk then asked about Kristine. They either remembered seeing her briefly or hadn't seen her at all and no one could tell him where Kristine was now.

Not good.

The closer he got to the doors the less sparse the crowd. A retired provincial court judge flagged him down, a friend of his father's, he could hardly refuse to stop and offer a few words. He kept his eyes on the crowd and catalogued the people drifting in and out of the room. They were exchanging courthouse rumors when a man stepped into the doorway. Caleb's heart stopped cold. When his gaze landed on Caleb he stopped searching and nodded his head. The skinhead.

Caleb excused himself. When he was within four feet of him he turned his back and led the way. Caleb pulled out his phone, his thumbs punching out the last couple of words to the message he'd drafted earlier to his friend with the Vancouver Police Department, he included the photo he'd taken earlier. He hit send and stuffed his phone in his pocket. Then once again he was climbing the broad staircase leading to the upper levels of the house. They paused in front of Jason's office. With a sneer he pushed open the door and motioned Caleb inside. Caleb hoped like hell the private investigator he'd hired knew his stuff and that the recording technology Zack Kincaid had set him up with was working.

Caleb stepped past him into Jason's office for the second time. Relief came quick at finding Sophie, pale, tense, but unhurt. The skinhead shut the door behind him and moved to stand against the wall to his left. Kristine was there sitting beside Sophie on the opposite side of the room. Jason lounged against the front of his desk, arms crossed. He tried hard for casual. And failed.

"Perfect. Enough time to figure out a few things before our announcement." Jason held his hand out to his wife. Kristine pressed into Sophie and grasped for her hand. His jaw tightened. His arm dropped.

"Jason, have you lost your mind?" Caleb stepped forward. So did the man to his left. He held up a hand to stop him and keep him in place. "What's this going to accomplish? Why are Kristine and Sophie here? This is between you and me."

"Not anymore. You involved my wife. You dragged Kristine into this." He stood full height and scowled in Caleb's direction. "This is your fault. All yours. What happens now is on you."

"Jason." Kristine tried to stand and wobbled. She put a hand out to catch the back of the couch. Tears flooded her eyes. "Stop it. Stop *this*."

"There's no need for any of this." Caleb moved in

Kristine's direction. Jason blocked his way. Caleb's phone buzzed in his pocket. He ignored it. His cue to send the police.

"I'm doing this as much for her, for our child, the future of our family." He kept his eyes on Caleb. There was no remorse in his voice, only purpose.

Child?

It was a hammer blow against any hope he had of reasoning with him. It changed everything. He looked to Kristine for confirmation. She bit down on her bottom lip, tears glistening in her eyes, head nodding in apology.

"Jesus, Jason." Caleb lifted his hands, palms open, heart on his sleeve. "All the more reason to let them go."

"Not until we come to an understanding."

Kristine put a hand over her mouth but her cry escaped through her shaking fingers.

"Here. Sit down. Try to stay calm." Sophie rose from the couch to support Kristine who swayed. She put her arms around her, hugged her close. Her worried eyes went from him to Drummond. "She needs medical attention. You have to get her to a hospital. Now."

God, he was so in love with her. So much it hurt. And because he did he feared for her. So much it paralyzed him. He struggled, pushed to find his reason and a way to stall until the police arrived. "Listen to her, Jason. Let them go."

"When I hear advice from a real doctor I'll take it."

Enough.

"Do not be so fucking stupid you can't see what's happening right in front of you. It's over." His words stabbed the air. The wrong words. Careless words.

"You're done."

Jason advanced until they were nose to nose. "I've had just about enough of your threats for one evening."

"You heard Sophie. Kristine needs medical attention. If you do not want to lose this child too…" Caleb gritted his teeth. He had Jason's attention right where he wanted it. On him. "Let. Them. Go."

His whiskey soaked breath was a whisper in his face. "You are a dead man."

"Yeah?" Caleb worked up a sneer while counting seconds in his head.

"Oh, yeah." Jason searched his face, lips parted, teeth showing.

"I'm fine." Kristine pushed up from the couch and moved in their direction. Or tried to, before Sophie grabbed onto her arm. "There's no need to hurt anyone. Please."

"See, she's fine." But Jason's lips thinned. He backed up. "She comes from strong stock after all. The Lincolns are nothing if not hearty folk."

"You have me. You don't need them."

"Ever the self-sacrificing type. It's getting old, Caleb. You've already got the girl, no need to impress her. As for Kristine, her place is with me. Always. 'Til death do us part."

At those words Kristine slipped back down onto the couch. Sophie sat down beside her. She put a hand to Kristine's forehead then her cheek. "She needs to go to the hospital. For the sake of your child she needs to go now."

Caleb glanced at the bald man to his left. His jacket was open, gun holster easily accessible. His hands clasped in front of his body. Eyes eager. Avid. Strained with waiting.

"Caleb and Sophie are going for a ride." Jason consulted his watch. He nodded at his man who drew his gun. Then he motioned to Kristine. "You and I have an announcement to make."

Kristine stared at him horrified. "No."

"Yes." Jason lunged for Kristine who shrank back against the couch. Sophie, being Sophie, tried to block him from his wife. He slapped her. She slapped back.

Caleb was forced to turn his back on Jason and move to stop the skinhead who charged in their direction.

The skinhead yanked out his gun. "Not another step."

Caleb eyed the gun. He put up his hands and shifted. His sole intention to block the women from his view. He tracked the man's eye movements and stepped in time to them. He paid attention to the sounds behind him. Another slap. A grunt. Kristine's cry.

"Out of my way." The skinhead tried to shove past him.

From behind an arm wrapped around Caleb's throat. He stumbled under Jason's weight.

"Call her off, Caleb." Jason's breath was hot against his ear.

Caleb latched onto Jason's arm and yanked. His grip loosened a fraction and he sucked air into his lungs. He stumbled when Jason swung them around and he grabbed for something to hold on to. His fist closed around a handful of fabric. The lapel of a jacket.

A loud crack split the air, hung there suspended. It was an effort to lift his arms to try and cover his ears.

Pain.

The shape of the man in front of him blurred. Jason's chokehold loosened, but not enough. The floor came up to meet them both. Jason landed in a heap beside him. Caleb stared at the ceiling, tried to catch his breath.

"No." Sophie's panicked cry worried him. No— What? What now? Then he heard his name.

His side. Something was wrong with his side. It hurt.

"Sit here. I don't need you collapsing too."

Sophie's voice. Did it mean she was okay? He lifted his head but got distracted by the wet, warm, sticky stuff covering his hand. He was leaking blood.

Oh, shit.

"But he's hurt." Kristine's voice.

Black crept in around the edges of his vision. He swallowed and concentrated on the voices. God, he was going to throw up.

"I know, but you're in my way. Someone call 911. Now."

Sophie sank down beside him. "Let me see."

She undid his tuxedo jacket with frightening efficiency. Buttons popped off his shirt, the tails of it sliding free of his pants. He focused on her face because none of the panic he was feeling showed there, not one scrap. It calmed him until she frowned.

"Not so bad but bad enough. I need towels. Kristine? Get me towels."

When she didn't reply Sophie shot her a frustrated look. Caleb watched her reaction and wished he hadn't. He turned his head to see Kristine hovering over Jason staring down at hands covered in blood.

Sophie lunged. "Oh, shit. Shit. Shit. Shit."

She pushed Kristine to the side. He watched as she stripped Jason of his pants. Blood spurted. He gagged and turned away.

Other voices in the background. Hard to say who. He didn't recognize any of them. But they seemed insistent on giving Sophie updates on things like police, ambulances and who was coming.

"Any minute. How are you doing? Caleb?"

No choice but to look in her direction again. "Fine. Don't worry."

"The paramedics will be here any second." Her hands covered Jason's wound. Even he could see it wasn't having much effect. She pressed harder and his body jerked. People closed in, hovered. "Anyone who's not a paramedic or a doctor needs to get the hell out of this room."

More shuffling and mumbling. Low pitched demands.

"Out." Other than her brief order she ignored the spray of shock reverberating around the room.

Kristine hunched down on Jason's other side and grabbed her husband's hand. "Don't worry."

"Bleeding's not stopping," warned Sophie.

"I'm...sorry." It was a whisper in the air.

Kristine leaned in. "Don't talk."

"Never...meant...to...leave...you."

"Damn it." Sophie yelled at Jason. "Don't you die on me, you asshole."

The background babble twisted around them. Confusion. Gasps.

Kristine stifled a cry. "It's going to be okay."

"Call...your Dad...contain...things."

She sniffed back tears. "Don't worry about that

right now."

"Our…baby."

"No. No, you don't." Sophie grabbed Kristine's hand and instructed her to press down. She scrambled over to Caleb. "This is going to hurt."

Pain sliced through his side. His belt buckle was in her hands and sliding through the loops of his pants before he knew what was happening.

"What are you doing?" Kristine held onto Jason, panic thickening her voice. "Sophie?"

Sophie scrambled out of his line of vision. He stretched his neck, pain radiated out from his side. He flinched but caught sight of Sophie on Jason's other side pushing Kristine back.

"Tourniquet."

That's when he knew things were bad. Last result bad. He tried to get to his knees. Pain blurred the edges of his vision. But he needed to help. To do something besides bleed all over the floor.

"Stay right where you are, Caleb. Don't you dare move. Or faint. I can only deal with one thing at a time."

His ears weren't working. He heard his name through a bag of cotton. A sliver of panic ran through him. He shook it off.

"Caleb."

He heard her. They probably heard her in the hallway.

"Caleb."

Real loud. Again. He tried to nod and managed a word. "Yeah."

He sat back down.

"Stay," she yelled.

And then the cavalry arrived. Someone called out. A hand on his shoulder.

"Two gunshot victims...femoral artery...abdominal..." And things started to fade to black...

****

Sophie assisted the ambulance attendants hoisting Caleb onto a stretcher.

She wanted to smooth a hand over his cheek but hers were smeared with blood. "I'll be there as soon as I can."

"We're ready to go," said the attendant.

Sophie straightened and watched them wheel him out. Then he was out of sight. She offered up a silent prayer. They wouldn't know the extent of the damage until they got him to the hospital.

He could have died.

She shivered. Didn't want to remember. Did not want to look behind her and remember how close she'd come to losing him. One body for the coroner was enough. Despite Jason Drummond's crimes she hadn't wished him dead. But dead he was.

She worked to steady her breathing, to control the residuals of panic and adrenaline. Kristine was sitting on a chair off to the side with a paramedic next to her. He leaned down and said something to her. She shook her head and clutched at the blanket someone had laid over her shoulders.

Sophie crossed the room. "Kristine, you need to go get checked out."

Her eyes never strayed from the body of her husband. "No, I should stay with..."

Sophie urged her up and off the chair. "We'll take

care of him, I promise."

"You'll stay? With him?"

She was saved from answering by an older gentleman who rushed to their side. He pulled Kristine into a mammoth hug and pulled her gaze away from the body on the floor. "Oh my God, what the hell happened? Are you okay, sweetie pie?"

"Daddy?"

"It's me. I'm here." His worried eyes searched Sophie's face. "Is she okay?"

"She needs to go to the hospital, get checked out." Sophie nodded at the white-haired gentleman. "We're having trouble convincing her to go."

Kristine's father gave a gruff nod. "Come on, sweetie. Come with me."

"Jason?"

He glanced at Sophie and she shook her head. His gaze went to the floor and he quickly averted it. "We'll talk about it on the way to the hospital. Come away now. And let them take care of him."

Sophie sighed. Sobs sounded in the hallway. Not Kristine, but new ones followed by a different gentleman's gruff voice, loud and demanding. She was so tired and all she wanted was to go to Caleb.

"Dr. Monroe? A few questions." The police officer held out her hand. "Constable Shreve."

Sophie held up her hands. "As long as I can wash up first."

"Of course. There's a bathroom down the hall a ways. I'll take you. There's quite the crowd assembled out there."

She nodded her thanks. Out in the hall an older gentleman clutched onto an older woman bent over with grief. Others huddled around the periphery. He demanded answers. His face red. His words angry.

The policewoman opened the door to washroom and Sophie slipped inside. The door closed behind her and she breathed in the quiet. She stepped up to the sink, turned on the hot water tap. She stared at the ravaged woman in the mirror.

"I did everything I could. There wasn't anything else I could have done. Nothing," she whispered.

Was there?

****

Caleb struggled to open his eyes. Windows. They surrounded him. A glass room.

Right.

His lids drifted close against his will. There was movement to his right. Someone covered his hand. Squeezed it.

A whisper.

"I'm here…"

The next time he opened them the images were sharper. More in focus. He noted the whsst of machines. The scrape of a chair. But his eyelids refused to obey his command to stay open. Cool fingers brushed his cheek. Sleep beckoned and he gave over to the seduction.

****

Hospitals were loud. And bright. Caleb lifted a hand to cover his eyes. Pain travelled up his side. He let it drop. Tried to shift position. Abandoned the idea.

"Go back to sleep. It's the best medicine."

Sophie.

"You're here." He cleared his throat. It didn't help. He tried again. "Kristine?"

"She's fine. Don't worry, she's in good hands." She frowned, her gaze on the various machines at the side of his bed. She hummed as she studied them. Then she looked at him, her smile small. Tired. "How are you feeling?"

"What happened?" He struggled to remain awake.

"You had surgery, but everything's fine. Go to sleep."

He was afraid to ask the unimaginable. The silence stretched.

She straightened his covers, smoothed them out. Checked the position of his call button. He grabbed for her hand. He knew the answer, but he wanted confirmation. "Jason?"

Her look was stark. "He didn't make it."

Not nightmares but the truth. He needed to get out of this bed.

"Kellie and Quinn?" He ignored the pain and struggled to sit up."

"They're fine." She put her hands on his shoulders and with little effort guided him back down. "You're not going anywhere. You've just had surgery, for crap sakes."

"Great…bedside manner." But he was embarrassed by his weakness so he shut his eyes and invited the darkness.

When he opened them again he was alone. He had no idea of the time much less the day. A nurse came into the room, a smile on her face.

"Look who's awake." She stuck a digital thermometer in his mouth. Popped it out.

"When can I leave?"

She fussed with his IV, her soft laugh floated

around the room. "You'll being enjoying the delights of our stellar accommodations for at least another couple of days."

"No, seriously?"

She patted her shoulder. "Don't worry we'll take good care of you."

"Great."

"Cheer up, it could have been much, much worse. The only thing the bullet hit was muscle. Say a prayer of thanks it didn't enter your abdominal cavity. A couple of weeks and you'll be feeling much better."

"A couple of weeks?" He didn't have the luxury of time. A shit storm was coming with Sophie, Kellie, and Quinn at the center of it. "I need to talk to the doctor."

"Don't we all."

"Can't you call him? Get him in here?"

"Honey, best thing you can do is relax. He'll be here when he gets here." She straightened his covers. He suffered through more of her explanations about what to expect and didn't hear half of it. It tired him out to think about it. He stared at the ceiling after she left. No cell phone. No computer. No access. Nothing else to do. But sleep.

The silence woke him up. Like a nightmare. He willed his eyes open. A hand closed over his. One he'd recognize anywhere even without the accompanying waft of Chanel No. 5. She bent over to give him a kiss on the cheek.

"Welcome back, honey."

He smiled at her, thankful to find his mouth worked better, his eyes clearer. "Mom."

His dad appeared at her side and put a hand on her shoulder. She left it there, offered his father a small smile. Caleb blinked.

"Dad?"

"Yes, son." Joseph "Joe" Quinn patted his hand.

His parents? Side by side. Touching. That couldn't mean good things.

"Has something else happened? What's wrong?"

"Nothing! You're going to be fine." His mother gave him her best shocked silly frown.

"But you'd tell me if something was…not right?"

"Of course, son."

He breathed a sigh of relief. "Okay, just checking."

"They're finally letting us stay more than a few minutes."

"Great." He glanced around the room. No Sophie. "That's great."

His mother turned at the sound of footsteps. "Sophie, there you are."

His father pulled her forward into their little group, his smile proud. "He's awake. I think he's out of the woods. What's my favorite doctor think?"

"Oh, he's going to be fine. Don't worry." Sophie laughed and the small hoops in her ears danced.

She was in one piece. She was beautiful. She was here. Caleb's heart stuttered. He hoped it wasn't obvious on the monitor. He half-expected to hear alarms go off. "Good to know. I'm a little fuzzy on the details."

"You're a hero." His mother squeezed his hand.

Sophie snorted.

"We'll let Sophie give you the details. We've already heard them." He laughed and looked to his ex-wife. "I'll buy you a coffee?"

His mother hesitated before giving in and lifting a

hand. "Fine. But we'll be back."

Caleb stared at their retreating backs. "What kind of drugs am I on?"

She bit her bottom lip. "Why?"

"How..."

She took pity on him. "Apparently, your getting shot has created a truce. But, believe me, it wasn't pretty at first."

"I hope it lasts. I don't plan on repeating the experience."

Sophie dropped down into the chair beside his bed and glared at him. "You scared the shit out of me."

"How...what happened with Jason?"

She gave it to him straight. "You were shot in the side. The bullet passed through and hit Jason in the leg. The femoral artery. He bled out."

"Shit."

She averted her eyes. "There was nothing I could do."

He frowned and reached for her hand. "Hey. You did everything you could. More. It's not your fault."

She nodded her head, the movement abstract. "The shooter took off. They haven't found him yet."

"When can I get out of here?" It had to be soon. She was collapsing under the weight of grief, not enough sleep or food, too much stress. She'd go until she dropped.

"It won't be too long. With no complications you should be out in a few days."

"Marnie's funeral?"

"Is the day after tomorrow."

He had two days. Either the doctor would release him or he'd check himself out. "Jason's?"

"No word yet. But I'm pretty sure I'm not listed as need to know. I'm just stopping in before I go home to check on Kellie and Quinn, finish up the arrangements for Marnie's…funeral, clear things at the clinic so I can take a couple of days." She avoided his gaze. "I won't be back to see you before you're released."

He didn't like the sound of her voice. At all. She was slipping away. He was stuck in a hospital bed while she bore the weight of the world.

"Don't do this." Frustration swelled. "Don't shut me out."

"I need some time to myself." When her eyes met his he was hypnotized by the pain there. Trapped by it. "I'll be in touch in a couple of days."

Her tread was soft. She made no noise. Just drifted through the door without looking back. He let his head fall back on his pillow. Was it madness to think he could make it better for her? To wish he could be everything to her? Defeat was a bitter pill he refused to swallow. He wasn't giving up. When he was released he was heading in her direction.

****

Sophie held court at the front of the room, her plate of food untouched, her coffee cold. Beside her was the small table holding the urn of ashes, a bouquet of flowers, and two framed pictures of Marnie. It was more of a wake than a funeral, but she figured Marnie would have wanted laughter, people milling about, more mess than stiff and somber. She would have enjoyed the pun too. There was no booze served, but coffee flowed along with the stories.

They came from all over to pay their last respects. The Pacific coast had blessed Vancouver with lovely weather and bits of sunshine. It made travel easier. They walked, bussed, or caught a ride with friends to get here. It was a chance to pay their respects to the best Finder in decades. They milled about, stacked food on plates, gripped cups in their hands.

Many of them were patients of hers, her clinic staff, of course, and the few friends she'd found the time to make were also in attendance. Kellie was there, pretty in the new clothes they finally found the time to shop for, and pushing Quinn in his stroller. Without the two of them, the last couple of days would have driven her mad. Pulled in six different directions, she'd slept little and eaten less.

This morning she'd woken up dizzy and disorientated. It was the push she needed to seek help. She made an appointment with a grief counselor. Her relationship with her sister had contained too much baggage, too much dysfunction, for her to overcome her grief on her own. She needed to put the past behind her, to learn how to remember her sister without the crushing load of guilt. Making the appointment was her first proactive step toward recovering her life.

She missed sane. She missed the certainty of knowing what she wanted. And while her life had never been calm, or neat, it had been governed by her purpose. Her choices.

Then along came Caleb.

She didn't feel like Caleb was a choice. He was more of a necessity. All the time she'd been working on Jason she'd been thinking about him. Worrying about Caleb. The thought of losing him had terrified her. For two days she'd gone over every second of the last moments of Jason Drummond's life trying to determine if her feelings and concern for Caleb had compromised her focus. Dulled her edge.

"Hey, Doc."

She snapped back to the present and held out a hand. "Thanks for coming, David."

He nodded and moved on. The man behind him stepped forward. "I'm awfully sorry about your sister. She was a good woman."

Sophie smiled. "Thank you."

"No problem, ma'am." He flipped off his tattered ball cap. "She never got tired of bragging about her little sister, the doctor. She was mighty proud of you."

Tears welled in her eyes and she blinked them back. It wasn't the first time she'd heard those sentiments today. "Thank you. That means a lot to me."

And it did. It meant everything.

The line continued to pass by her. They shared stories of a sister she'd never known. Not really. Too busy trying to save her, she'd sacrificed getting to know her. She'd never let it be a two-way street, never allowed Marnie to help her back. She saw her mistake now it was too late. For no reason she thought of the night they'd all shared pizza. Normal. Marnie snarking. Kellie laughing. Caleb all dorky charm. And her? She'd felt lighter despite their circumstances. That night had been a gift.

The line thinned with only a few stragglers left. The door at the back of the room opened and Caleb limped in as exceptionally dressed as ever. He joined the queue bringing up the rear, his movements slow and careful. He chatted to the older woman in front of him. Kellie came over and gave him a gentle hug. She'd missed him too. With his hand pressed against his side, he bent down to run a hand over Quinn's tiny head before straightening and giving the inquiring woman in front of them some crazy explanation. She knew it was ridiculous because she laughed and waved his words away. He was like a chameleon. He fit here too.

And in her bed.

In her heart.

But did she fit in his?

His gaze met hers and his lips curved upwards. Smiling was second nature to him, laugh lines fanned out from the corner of his eyes. Her heart squeezed. He winked. The choke hold of grief lessened the tiniest bit. Her lips lifted in return.

She spoke to the last mourner while her staff finished handing out the packaged up leftovers. They offered brown paper bag lunches containing sandwiches, pieces of fruit, muffins and cookies. They filled to-go cups with either coffee or tea and fitted them with lids. A take-away meal for those in need of it.

A couple of minutes later there were fewer than a dozen people left in the room. Peggy, her receptionist, put an arm around her waist and pulled her close. "We're pretty much finished up here. Do me a favor?"

Sophie let her head fall against Peggy's shoulder and nodded.

"He wants to comfort you. Let him."

Lips brushed her hair followed by another squeeze to her middle, then she was gone. It wasn't hard to find Caleb. He passed the time with Kellie. When he glanced her way she tried a smile. He put a hand on the back of Kellie's arm, said something. She kissed his cheek and went to help her staff.

All of a sudden she couldn't wait for this day to end. To be out of the sterile room with its white walls, beige floor, and utilitarian tables and chairs. The quiet echoed. She wanted to be home. With Caleb.

There was no time to figure it out. She bit her lip. "Hi."

"Hey there." He didn't reach out to touch her.

She pushed her regret aside. He was here. Despite the pain that showed in the lines around his mouth, his shadowed eyes. "I can't believe they discharged you."

"They didn't."

She choked back a laugh. "Figures. I'm still glad you came."

"Time to go?" he asked.

She nodded. "You'll follow me?"

He smiled. "Anywhere you want."

So Caleb. Casual. Effortless. Appealing.

****

Caleb pointed out the house to the taxi driver. He drew in a careful breath and blew it out. It didn't help. Pain dogged every little movement. He pulled out his wallet and paid the driver. The slow slide out of the car took everything out of him. He had no choice but to reach into his pocket for the little bottle of prescription pain pills. He swallowed one down. The path to her door looked impossibly long. He concentrated. One foot in front of the other. Over and over again. Sophie opened the door and waited. He straightened up.

"Idiot."

She mumbled it, but he was pretty sure he hadn't mistaken the word. He held up his hand to stop her from coming down the steps. "I've got this. Don't worry about me."

She stepped back as he made his way up the walk. "You should be in bed."

"I never thought I'd say this to a beautiful woman but I'm tired of being in bed." He braced his hand against the doorframe.

"Sorry we just kind of dropped everything." She shifted things around, Quinn's stroller, a cardboard box of stuff, a bag of Quinn's things, and made a path into her living room. She held out a hand. "Here let me help you."

He waved her off. "I'm good."

"Liar." She reached down and picked up a baby toy up off the floor. Placed it safely out of the way. From somewhere inside, Kellie squealed and exclaimed over something Quinn had done. Sophie laughed and followed the sound of her voice.

He wanted to rush in and see what it was, to find out what the little guy had done.

In the next moment he wondered why? How exciting could it be? He was five days old. But it didn't matter. As his surrogate father, he should be there. He wanted to be included in this weird little family dynamic—thing.

It should freak him the hell out, but it didn't. At all. More lights went on inside her place. Despite the harsh reality of the day's goodbyes her place glowed with welcome. Beckoned.

He liked to think his place had a certain appeal. He loved it. And she didn't even know why or where he lived. What would she think of his condo? His art collection? His view of the water? She had no idea he loved the sea. That he was a member of the Vancouver Rowing Club. That he recycled.

He wanted to take the next step with her. To show her his life. She'd already met his parents. They adored her on sight. He'd suffered through two days of interrogation, his mother wanted details on everything little thing. It was the other reason he'd insisted on going home. And the reason they let him. Sympathy.

Sophie stuck her head around the corner. "You okay?"

"Yep. Dandy."

"I'm just going to change."

"Not a problem." In fact it was perfect. With Sophie in her bedroom he searched out Kellie. He found her heating a bottle for Quinn, juggling baby, formula and bottle like a pro.

He tapped Quinn's tiny fist. "Hey there, big guy."

Kellie gave him a quick glance. "Is it okay to ask what's going to happen to Quinn and me? Now that he's dead?"

"It's always okay to ask questions. In fact you should insist on asking them. I'm your lawyer. You can ask me anything. Anytime."

"Okay, what happens now? With child support, I mean?"

The tricky part. "Jason died before signing any papers. In regards to Quinn there's nothing in writing to stipulate what happens in the event of his death. There's no clause in his will specifying payment. No court order. So I'll make a petition to his estate claiming unpaid child support as a debt. His estate will look after it."

"God, everything is such a mess. Sophie said me and Quinn can stay here for as long as we need, but I don't want to freeload forever."

"I don't want you to worry. You'll both be looked after. I promise." If Jason's estate didn't look after it he would. That was the easy part.

She offered him a smile. It trembled at the corners, her pent up worry escaping in a little puff of breath. "Okay, I feel better. Thanks." She went up on her tiptoes and kissed his cheek.

The scent of baby and candy-flavored lip gloss wrapped around his heart and squeezed. He cleared his throat. "We need to finalize the housesitting details. You still up for it?"

"It's freaking me out, but yeah."

"Did you get something to eat?" He reached up into a cupboard to pull out one of Sophie's endless cans of soup. The pain made him wince.

She popped the bottle in Quinn's mouth. "No. I wasn't super hungry."

He searched for the can opener. "How are things around here?"

Kellie sighed. "Quiet. And weird."

He opened a cupboard and pulled out the bread for toast. "How's she doing?"

Kellie shot a brief glance down the hallway before shrugging her shoulders. "I don't know, lost? Tired. But she's holding it together, know what I mean?"

He nodded. "I do. How about you? How are you doing?"

"It sucks, but I'm hanging in there. It helps to have Quinn." Arms full of baby she headed into the living room area and settled on the sofa.

He set the pot on the stove and turned the heat down to low. A hockey game was on TV so he joined Kellie on the sofa, settled back against the cushions.

"Will you be okay here for a while Friday night without Sophie?"

"Sure." She shrugged. "Why?"

He smiled. "I've got a plan."

Kellie grinned back. "Don't worry, Quinn and I can hold down the fort for one night. We'll have a party. Raise the roof."

"Ha, ha."

"Seriously, go for it. She so needs a break." She looked down at Quinn, blew him a kiss. "And as scary as it seems, Quinn and I need to get used to being on our own."

Sometimes wisdom and courage came packaged in five feet two inches of teenage girl.

When Sophie emerged from her room they ate chicken noodle soup and buttered toast. The conversation was careful. No one had the energy for anything heavy. Once they were done, he insisted on cleaning up the kitchen. There was some huffing and puffing, but in the end Sophie let him. When he was done he called a cab. He insisted Sophie stay where she was rather than see him to the door. He handed her a sheet of paper.

"My address. Friday night how about I make you dinner at my place? Seven o'clock."

She looked at him in confusion with the beginnings of a refusal on her lips.

"I cleared it with the boss." He winked at Kellie, kissed Sophie on the cheek and backed up. "Don't over think. Come."

****

Sophie fantasized about cancelling. She fantasized about going. About Caleb. Rumpled sheets and sex. It was tempting to give in to her insecurities and retreat, but it was also gutless. And lonely. She wasn't going to honor her sister's memory by choosing the easy way out.

"How about these?" Kellie held up a pair of large hooped earrings. She jangled them. "Sexy."

"I've never worn them." Sophie shrugged off her doubts, wishing Kellie's excitement was contagious and reached for the earrings.

"Perfect." Kellie's head bobbed in excitement. "What do you think he's planning?"

"I don't know." Sophie frowned when Kellie pulled open her underwear drawer. "Maybe I should pick out my own bra?"

Kellie held up a pair of cotton panties. "Really?"

"They were on sale."

"Sweet. This is more like it." She shoved the other pair back in and pulled out the lacy, black lingerie Sophie had bought to wear on Christmas Eve. She held it up and danced it around.

"So glad you approve." Sophie laughed and snatched them out of Kellie's hand. "For the record, I can dress myself."

Kellie ignored her and walked over to her open closet. She ran her fingers over the black dress hanging off the door. "Okay, the dress is a given. What about shoes? Please tell me you have some heels stashed in there along with all those nasty work crocs and running shoes?"

Sophie rolled her eyes. She reached up and pulled a box down from the top of her closet and handed it her.

Kellie pulled the lid off, tossed it aside. Out came a sandal with a four inch stab-you-through-the-heart heel and a couple of thin straps. She held it up. "Shut up, these are fabulous."

She'd see what happened when she put them on. "Here's hoping I don't break my ankle."

"Small steps, heel to toe." Kellie stuffed the shoe back inside and shoved the box back at Sophie. "You'll be fine."

Sophie raised her eyebrows.

"What?"

"I didn't know you were such a fashionista."

She shrugged. "I read magazines."

"Hey." Sophie put a hand on her arm, dipped her head hoping to catch Kellie's eye. "Is that what you're interested in? Fashion?"

"I don't know. Maybe. I like getting all dressed up, you know?" Her head went down and she took great care in studying the carpet of Sophie's bedroom. "But I've always kinda wanted to try interior design. To create fabulous spaces. To think in color."

Sophie put a finger under Kellie's chin and guided it up. "If that's what you want, then I'm going to do everything I can to help make it happen. I promise. And not because of Marnie, although she'd haunt me if I didn't, but because you and Quinn have come to mean a great deal to me. I like to think we can be sisters of a sort."

"I'd like that." Her smile was shy, her eyes full. "More than anything I'd like that."

"Oh God, having a moment. Nope, not going to tear up." Sophie waved a hand back and forth in front of her eyes. "I have no idea if this mascara is waterproof."

"Then don't you dare." Kellie's laugh wobbled.

"Come on, let's get you ready and out the door. Caleb is going to freak when he sees you."

The cab ride to Caleb's was torture. Should she? Shouldn't she? She was a daisy being plucked clean of her reason. It was annoying. She wasn't a waffler. She was a doer. By the time the taxi dropped her off outside the glass doors of 1515 Homer Street in Kings Landing, she was the one freaking out. She glanced way up, then down the street, over to the seawall, which of course was right outside his door. He didn't have money, he had MONEY.

Crap on a stick.

You didn't acquire an address in the revamped warehouse district without some serious bucks. False Creek was right there, Granville Island across the way. She'd bet her lacy, black panties the view from above was incredible. And keep her panties every time because no one would bet against a sure thing.

She peered through the glass into the marble foyer. Of course, there was a concierge. Any second someone was going to walk out the front door carrying a little dog in a purse. She didn't do little dogs. Or yoga. Or the color pink.

Then again she was passing time on the street teetering on stilts and wearing Victoria's version of underwear which was so lacking in any kind of substance she was this close to going commando. Maybe yoga wasn't such a bad idea. If she had any kind of zen going on right now she wouldn't be such a mess.

Over a guy.

Well, not just any guy.

Over Caleb.

Because he was The One.

She felt it in her bones. And other damp places.

Her eyes travelled up, up, up, up. He was in there somewhere waiting. She squared her shoulders and went through the hoops needed to gain entrance, found the elevator and rode it to the top. She ran sweaty palms over her gently-used evening coat. The elevator doors opened. This was crazy. She snorted. More like insane. She stepped out and followed the numbers. A door opened and Caleb stepped out into the hall.

Heaven help her, he looked fresh and damp from a shower. Black dress pants, dark dress shirt, sleeves turned up to the elbows and undone at the throat.

Heel. Toe. Heel. Toe.

You're committed. Do not fall flat on your face.

The corners of his mouth lifted. Her breath hitched. You couldn't fake a smile like his. He moved back to let her past and she slid by without tripping over her feet. Or tongue.

"Let me take your coat."

She shrugged out of it to reveal the dress she'd bought for his company's fundraiser. The one she'd ditched what seemed like a million years ago. She smoothed a hand over the sleeveless, knee-length dress high in the front and very low in the back as she surveyed his personal space.

She glanced back over her shoulder intending to compliment him, but he was holding her coat and staring, a stunned look on his incredible face. Everything in her relaxed. The dress, the jewelry, the lingerie. The shoes. She was thankful for all of the props. They gave her the confidence to meet his hungry look with a what-are-you-going-to-do-about-it look of her own.

He tossed her coat over the hallway table. A laugh bubbled out of her as she backed up. She didn't get far. He caught her. His casual smile was gone. Intensity burned in his eyes, his hands smoothed over her hair and down her back.

"I missed you." It was more accusation than entreaty.

"And."

He took it as the challenge it was meant to be and captured her mouth. Sensation swamped her chasing away the cold, the cloying sadness, the guilt, and it felt so very good to be free of it for even a moment. She felt alive. Her need bubbled up like lava waiting to spill out and devour everything in its path. She met his tongue bold stroke for bold stroke.

He pulled away and rested his forehead against hers. "That was a lot like getting shot, only in a good way."

All of a sudden she was hungry. Not starving. Not desperate. But ready to eat. The dining room table was covered with linens and bold white dishes, silverware and flowers. Wine glasses, water glasses, all artfully arranged. It was beautiful. And it was for her. "You've gone to a lot of trouble."

He moved in close. His warm fingers squeezed hers as he lifted her hand to his lips. He led her over to the table, pulled out a chair. "It occurred to me we may have skipped a few steps. Drinks. Supper at a restaurant. Candles and wine. Popcorn in movie theaters. A little backtracking was in order, but I didn't think you were ready for the whole going-out-in-public deal. So I hope this makes up for some of it. I didn't plan on accosting you the minute you walked in the door. But that dress…"

She sat down, thankful to be off her feet. "Was bought with the express purpose of kicking your butt the night of the fundraiser."

"Consider my ass properly kicked."

She leaned back, checked out the space beyond the dining area. Art hung from the interior walls, most abstract, all gorgeous. The furniture more inviting than arranged. A stack of books over there. Requisite big screen TV. Jazz drifted out from invisible speakers. The view was stunning.

"So what do you think of the place?"

"It gorgeous. A girl could get used to this."

"The only person I care about getting used to anything is you." And the question was there in his eyes.

Her lips parted. And closed. Insecurities clogged her throat. But then she thought of all the time she'd lost with her sister. Because she'd been stubborn. And single-minded. Afraid. So, she blurted it out. "I think I'm in love with you."

His lips curved. "That simplifies things because I'm pretty sure I love you too."

Hearing his words settled her stomach. The way he said them settled her heart. They gave her the courage to be honest. "Things are bound to settle down. But I can't promise you normal. Or easy. Or even my undivided attention. There will be times when I won't be—"

He leaned in close. "So we see how things go. We'll fit the Easter egg hunts and pumpkin carving around the marches and rallies. We'll work on balancing careers and who spends what night where.

And then we'll reevaluate what doesn't work. We'll figure it out together."

She held those words to her heart. Let the warmth and relief seep all the way in. She ached with want. For him. "Together."

His fingers trailed from her cheek to her collarbone, across her shoulder. Warm lips found the tender spot behind her ear. She wanted to drown in the pleasure of it all. Her skin pebbled under his touch. Her neck stretched. She lifted her hand. His hair was soft under her hand and a little damp from his shower. Her sigh was soft as her lips moved to find his.

"To the next part of the journey." His lips met hers.

A word about the author...

I grew up on a farm in the middle of Canada's breadbasket. Under the canopy of crisp blue prairie skies I read books. Lots and lots of books. Occasionally, I picked up a pen and paper or tapped out a few meager pages of a story on a keyboard and dreamed of becoming a writer when I grew up. One day I knew without question the time was right. What to write was never the issue—romance and the gut-wrenching journey toward forever.

I love to hear from and interact with readers! You can drop me a note at: karyngoodauthor@gmail.com

Or find me at: http://www.karyngood.com/

Other Karyn Good titles
available from The Wild Rose Press, Inc.:

BACKLASH

Thank you for purchasing
this publication of The Wild Rose Press, Inc.
For other wonderful stories of romance,
please visit our on-line bookstore at
www.thewildrosepress.com.

For questions or more information
contact us at
info@thewildrosepress.com.

The Wild Rose Press, Inc.
www.thewildrosepress.com

To visit with authors of
The Wild Rose Press, Inc.
join our yahoo loop at
http://groups.yahoo.com/group/thewildrosepress/